Praise for Rabindranath Maharaj

Fatboy Fall Down

"Heavy yet rewarding, Maharaj's novel is a reminder that resilience takes many forms—and that most exceed our naming." —*Kirkus Reviews*

The Amazing Absorbing Boy

"Sharply observed and entertaining . . . The language has a charming, natural ease, casually dropping articles and prepositions in a colloquial rhythm and delivering comic punchlines with dry, understated effect. But it is also a novel with deeper layers. At heart it is a rich exploration of the immigrant psychodrama of attraction and repulsion, welcome and paranoia, perception and misunderstanding." —*Toronto Star*

"Whatever the future holds, 'old' Regent Park survives in Maharaj's compelling new novel, *The Amazing Absorbing Boy*." —Mark Medley, *National Post*

"Samuel's ingenue-like innocence is very much to Maharaj's satiric purpose, like the innocence of Voltaire's *Candide*. Through that innocence we see the world—in this case, Toronto—in a fresh way [. . .] Maharaj never gives the feeling that he is crafting picturesque semi-comic figures merely to add colour to his narrative. These figures are both too enigmatic and too vivid for that. Samuel's first-person narrative itself produces an air of unreality in which the eccentrics fit right in." —Philip Marchand, *Open Book, National Post*

"In this charming literary novel, Trinidad-born Canadian Rabindranath Maharaj presents the fear and excitement of immigrating to Canada through the eyes of a 17-year-old Trinidadian teenager." —*Winnipeg Free Press*

"Maharaj superbly articulates the longing for home, on the one hand, and the dream of success in Canada on the other [. . .] an exhilarating interpretation of immigrant experience." —*Globe and Mail*

A Perfect Pledge

"*A Perfect Pledge* . . . will establish [Maharaj] as a major Canadian writer and literary figure of international stature . . . *A Perfect Pledge* shares the comically neutral tone of Naipaul's earlier novels, except that Maharaj's humour is broader, the characters more hilarious in their physical and linguistic excesses. Also, unlike Naipaul, Maharaj's mirth belies an implacable tenderness, an empathy and acceptance of human nature—a respectfulness that precludes scorn . . . In the end, we can't remember the precise moment we stopped rolling our eyes and began wiping them." —*The Globe and Mail*

"A poignant, studiously unsentimental portrait of a man too big for his community, and of the enduring bonds between father and son . . . What the book is, really, pure Maharaj. When a major writer emerges, the time for comparisons ends, and the time to celebrate the arrival of a distinctive, fully formed voice and sensibility begins." —*National Post*

"Among the many things to admire about *A Perfect Pledge* is the author's confidence . . . Imagine Don Quixote staying home in Trinidad, and you've got something like the wandering, witty, ultimately devastating story that Rabindranath Maharaj tells in *A Perfect Pledge* . . . This is a charming story . . . it's unstoppable . . . [with] a heartrending conclusion, tenderly, beautifully told . . . I'd advise keeping an eye out for more from Maharaj."
—*The Washington Post Book World*

"*A Perfect Pledge* delivers a beautifully written and beautifully sad tale."
—*Calgary Herald*

"For some time now—and especially with the release of *A Perfect Pledge*—literary critics have had a penchant for comparing Trinidadian author Rabindranath Maharaj to Trinidadian Nobel laureate V S Naipaul. Well, Naipaul he is not. With all due respect to international critics who stake such a claim, I beg to differ. Such a comparison is an insult to Maharaj. That is not to say that we should not be impressed that people are seeing Naipaul in Maharaj. After all, they're both Trini writers with East Indian roots, and they both are masters of characterisation. Still, Maharaj has worked painstakingly hard to establish his own voice as a writer . . . [he] is a literary magician who conjures up credible conflicts for characters." —*Trinidad Guardian*

"Maharaj has created a colourful universe of characters, and the writing is witty and sharp. Much like the Island of Trinidad, *A Perfect Pledge* is a polyglot of different styles. Part comedy, part tragedy, the book is Dickensian in scope, creates a detailed world of characters à la V S Naipaul and evokes the allegorical qualities of Chinua Achebe or even John Steinbeck. But it is those echoes of Don Quixote that linger the most." —*The Gazette* (Montreal)

"A sprawling, colorful epic . . . This novel's allure comes from its comic energy and its plucky, determined characters—especially the farmer's son, who struggles between his sense of filial duty and his desire for independence. In the end, the book is like a music box: it's charming and you have to admire its elaborate craftsmanship." —*The New York Times Book Review*

"What a delicious feeling it is to read the first pages of a 400-page book and know you are in the hands of an accomplished storyteller . . . It is impossible not to compare Rabindranath Maharaj with Nobel Prize-winning author V S Naipaul . . . This eminently satisfying novel has the clarity of Naipaul and some of the bite, and a great deal that is Maharaj's own." —*The Seattle Times*

The Lagahoo's Apprentice

"Fascinating, satisfying . . . *The Lagahoo's Apprentice* is dense and rich, and the apprentice of the title [is] one of the most fully realized characters I've come across in fiction . . . This is a very, very fine novel, wonderful reading for the women (and men) who've known a few lagahoos in their time."

—Elizabeth Nickson, *The Globe and Mail*

"A satisfying delight . . . it has a vivid sense of place, hilarious satire, Gothic mystery, [and] moments of wrenching poignancy . . . Maharaj triumphs . . ."

—*The Toronto Star*

"Maharaj's innumerable fresh and funny observations . . . define his style . . . Sympathetic, canny, and very entertaining." —*The Gazette* (Montreal)

"Observations are magnificently captured and enhance the mood of secrecy and gloom . . . Maharaj is a delicate craftsman with a compelling style . . . *The Lagahoo's Apprentice* is an accomplished novel." —*National Post*

"Maharaj indicates in a subdued but poignant way the corrosive effects of both colonialism and its outgrowth, neo-colonialism. One of the strengths of the novel, indeed, is its smooth integration of a great deal of the myth and recent history of the island and its people. In the process Maharaj, unlike V S Naipaul, demonstrates in his fiction that the present social, political, economic and even religious problems are outcomes of the days of colonialism, when the colonizer created 'mimic men', men with black skins but white masks. In this connection, time is a crucial theme in *The Lagahoo's Apprentice*. [. . . It] is a well-crafted novel. It is elegant in its language, and it successfully employs satire and humour to foreground the legacies of colonialism: fragmentation of identity, disillusionment, personal and political turmoil, nostalgia for a lost 'Eden', the persistent sense of futility and entrapment, and the problems of hybridity." —*Canadian Literature*

"Robin Maharaj compares very favorably to the older and more established Canadian writer of Caribbean origin, Austin Clarke. Both sing of remembered island paradises of poverty and passion, of lost parents, of exotic childhoods as sources of adult wisdom, of cultural dissonance which has at its roots personal disease. Both are masters of the English language they love to play with." —*January Magazine*

"Vivid, memorable . . . Against [a] bewitching, deftly conjured backdrop, Maharaj brings on a procession of angry, equivocal, caustically funny Trinidadian monologists." —*Quill & Quire*

Homer in Flight

"*Homer in Flight* . . . is an intelligent, balanced, deeply felt book . . . recommended reading for anyone seriously interested in what it means to be an immigrant rather than a tourist . . . Maharaj's eye for characterization is impeccable, as is his ability to find humour amid the grim, the sordid, and the dreary." —*Books in Canada*

"Rabindranath Maharaj is a talented and confident writer who has produced a work of unsparing vision and compassion . . . *Homer in Flight* is a riveting portrait of the immigrant tragedy . . . It is a novel that deserves a wide audience." —Neil Bissoondath, *Globe and Mail*

"A remarkable achievement, thematically and structurally . . . This novel has many attractions; it's a book that inspires admiration."
—Andre Alexis, *Toronto Star*

"Maharaj is skilled at inspiring sympathy for a protagonist whose blindnesses and mistakes he enjoys sending up. *Homer in Flight* is an artful, unpredictable, and entertaining addition to the literatures of both Canada and the Caribbean." —*Canadian Literature*

"Rabindranath Maharaj, like many cultural critics, has an unblinking, sardonic eye for the absurdities and hypocrisies that shape a society." —*Vancouver Sun*

The Interloper

"Rabindranath Maharaj is a breath of fresh air . . . His hope is infectious; his skill a pleasure; his stories a real awakening." —*Books in Canada*

"This book is wonderful! . . . The individual stories are rich and captivating. The whole is remarkable. Rabindranath Maharaj is a first-rate writer who deserves a wide readership and high acclaim." —*Halifax Chronicle-Herald*

"Some of the best Caribbean fiction these days is coming from the exiles, the writers who for one reason or another have settled in Toronto or New York or London and are torn between two worlds, between restlessness and nostalgia, ambition and roots . . . Maharaj writes with a welcome humour and irony, free of the overt bitterness and anger that sours so much writing from the diaspora." —*Caribbean Beat*

ALSO BY RABINDRANATH MAHARAJ

Novels

Fatboy Fall Down
Adjacentland
The Amazing Absorbing Boy
The Picture of Nobody
A Perfect Pledge
The Lagahoo's Apprentice
Homer in Flight

Short Stories

The Book of Ifs and Buts
The Writer and his Wife
The Interloper

Anthology

Luminous Ink (Co-editor)

A QUIET DISAPPEARANCE

STORIES

RABINDRANATH MAHARAJ

MAWENZI
HOUSE

We acknowledge the support of the Canada Council for the Arts for our publishing program. We also acknowledge support from the Government of Ontario through the Ontario Arts Council, and the support of the Government of Canada through the Canada Book Fund.

ONTARIO ARTS COUNCIL
CONSEIL DES ARTS DE L'ONTARIO
an Ontario government agency
un organisme du gouvernement de l'Ontario

Ontario

Canada Council for the Arts
Conseil des arts du Canada

Canada

Mawenzi House is a certified Benetech Global Certified Accessible™ (GCA) Publisher. The ebook version of this book meets GCA accessibility standards.

Cover design by Kavaitri Maharaj

"Broken Pieces" was previously published in *The Ampersand Review*;

"The Second Life" was previously published in *Fiddlehead.*

Library and Archives Canada Cataloguing in Publication

Title: A quiet disappearance : stories / Rabindranath Maharaj.

Names: Maharaj, Rabindranath, 1955- author

Identifiers: Canadiana (print) 20250161664 | Canadiana (ebook) 20250161672 | ISBN 9781774151839 (softcover) | ISBN 9781774151846 (EPUB) | ISBN 9781774151853 (PDF)

Subjects: LCGFT: Short stories.

Classification: LCC PS8576.A42 Q54 2025 | DDC C813/.54—dc23

Printed and bound in Canada by Coach House Printing

Mawenzi House Publishers
192 Spadina Ave, Suite 417
Toronto, ON, M5T 2C2
Canada

www.mawenzihouse.com

In memory of my sister, Auma

I should like to tidy things up and disappear.

VIRGINIA WOOLF

CONTENTS

A Quiet Disappearance

During my mother's funeral, I remember an old friend from another time telling me in her seedy room overflowing with one-eyed dolls somersaulting on purple pincushions that an unwanted child will forever wander the world like a grieving, restless ghost, searching for withheld love. And into this gap, she said, her sad face set against crimson slashes of crosses and daggers on her wall, we will pour all our hate because it's the only thing we understand.

I arrived late for the service and sat close to the back. In the front row, my sister had her arm around our father. I had not seen her in a year and my father in twice that period. I expected my sister, close to our mother, to be overwhelmed, but when she got up to deliver the eulogy, I was surprised at her composure. My father seemed to crumble in his seat.

Her gaze was on our father and I wondered if children like us could trace the hostility towards their parents to a singular searing moment—an unforgettable turn of betrayal and cruelty—or if it quietly germinated from minor acts of neglect adding up over the years and creeping out from all the dark corners until one day it solidified into a shadow that disfigured memories and made everything but the detestation irrelevant.

I remember a Grade 9 conversation about trips to cottages and Mexico. I was envious of these families with their anniversaries and holiday jaunts and the idea of reciprocity in all these parental investments. Resentment came like a flush of fever during each weekend visit to my mother, who had moved to Vaughan with my sister. It deepened during the hospital journeys after our mother was diagnosed with cancer. It was only on the day of her funeral, as I watched our father squirming in his seat, that I recognized its true form. Revulsion, pure and simple. And I knew, finally, to whom it was directed.

My sister, two years younger, had no idea. She did not share my shame of being wrenched from a familiar world and pushed into one where you were viewed as an undesirable. I knew my sister was sincere when she eulogized our mother, creating a fairy-tale parent, tender yet brave. "She had room for everyone in her heart," she said, and I thought of how different her upbringing had been from mine. When my father got up to speak, I slipped away and noticed a dozen mourners, unfamiliar men in black suits and women spidery inside their veils. At the end of the ceremony, hidden by the cypress tree where I had been smoking, I saw my father and sister looking around before they hugged and departed into their respective vehicles. I headed for the Kipling subway stop. At Kipling, I observed couples milling about, their gazes harsh and seeming to be directed at me. I decided to walk to High Park, which took me about two hours. When I eventually got to my apartment, I turned off my phone for the night and flopped into my bed. I slept uneasily, awakened several times by a muffled static sound as if someone were treading lightly on crepe. In the early morning, I saw several texts from my sister. The last, accompanied by undecipherable emojis, said, "Hey bro. Hope all is okay."

"I'm okay," I replied.

Following the funeral, I met her at The Ice Biscuit, a coffee shop near Exhibition station close to my apartment, at least thrice a year, and I listened quietly to her bubbly revelations of friends and diets and travelling plans. She was always bursting with new-fangled ventures, so I never brought up anything about our dead mother or distant father. Sometimes she would break off from her cheerful monologue to comment on my thinness or my smoking or my silence. The meetings were a chore, but I missed her optimism in the days afterwards. Once, she surprised me by stating that we were each a replica of a parent and I recalled my father murmuring that I couldn't be his son. It was my last year of high school and I had returned home late with the odour of marijuana on my clothes. I never mentioned this to my sister or anyone else.

The next time I saw my father, following the funeral, was the week after graduation from Ryerson. He called to state that he had some business downtown. My first inclination was to say I was busy, but I assumed his visit was connected to my graduation. I gave him directions to The Ice Biscuit. It had been two years since the funeral, so I was surprised at how much he had changed. His hair was thin at the crown and hung in stiff, unruly ringlets over his ears. He had gained weight, unevenly, and his lower jaw looked different somehow. Slacker and more recessed.

But if his appearance had altered, his attitude towards me remained the same. He asked about my journalism programme and when I mentioned a couple of courses I attended, I saw his hooded eyes examining the peacock patterns on the table and I wondered if he would even remember this conversation when he returned to his home in Whitby. I turned my attention away from him to a Tibetan family who seemed to be eating their muffins in slow motion. Their gestures were graceful and soft as if they had all the time in the world to plan and live and be happy.

My father shifted in his chair and I felt he was about to leave, but he asked what I intended to do now. I mentioned a job-posting in a community newspaper. That was not true; midway through my programme, I realized I had no genuine interest in journalism. I had submitted a few short stories to local magazines, I added. This *was* true. I saw the familiar look of disinterest and was curious why he was pretending any involvement in my life. Then he told me he had been to a few readings and there were never any faces like his. I assumed he was talking about older men, but he hunched forward and clasped his hands on the table and said that most Indian immigrants from the Caribbean were uninterested in art and literature. "They are peasants at heart," he pronounced in the singsong lilt he had never gotten rid of, and I wondered when this literary entry on his list of grievances had begun. "You are Indian, but not from India. From the Caribbean but not Black. Neither fish nor fowl." When he added I would never have an audience and would be isolated, I felt like saying that I had grown accustomed to that.

He grew silent, and I saw the thumb of one hand digging into the palm of the other. I got up. The Tibetan family was whispering to each other. The baby was dressed in a bonnet and frilly dress and the mother was loosely swinging its arms. From a distance, the child looked like a Victorian puppet. "I have to leave. Work."

He remained seated. "Still a tour guide?"

"I am a taxi dispatcher now." Any bit of guilt I felt at leaving the table vanished when I saw the disappointment on his face. It was only when I was back at work and checking my schedule that I realized that it was his birthday. Sixty-four or sixty-five. If it were the latter, he would probably be in line for retirement from his job as a supply teacher in Durham. I could have called my sister to verify his age, but she was teaching English in South Korea. Nevertheless, I marked the date on my calendar.

Eight months after that meeting "A Disappearance Foretold," a story I had submitted to a Toronto literary magazine was accepted. I felt like calling my father, which was odd because I knew how he would react. The story involved the visit of a young man to a farm five hours from the city. The narrator focused on the landscape and the sounds of the woods and an encounter with a drunken fisherman but nothing of the farmer and his family. No names, no clues he was an immigrant, no passages that explicitly expressed his disorientation. My father would notice this. In my mind, I could hear him commenting, "These faces are featureless, without identities or backgrounds."

I called him the following year on the date I had marked. There was no reply, and I wondered if he was out with the woman, a fellow teacher, who had been a frequent visitor when I was still at school and living with him. She was petite with fine features revealing no reassembling of her face, so she appeared much younger that first evening in the living room of the high-rise apartment from which my mother and sister had moved out the previous year.

She had come by weekly and they were both formal and restrained, so I was surprised when one night I returned early from band practice and saw them lying on the sofa, my father's face buried in her hair. One of her legs was on the sofa's backrest and my father was repeating, at intervals, muted sounds as if he were stumbling over a nursery rhyme. She was emitting a low hum, like the distant wheeze of a seabird. I tiptoed into my room and an hour later, I heard her car pulling out of the parking lot, and then the bathroom tap.

Apart from the fact that my father was on top of this woman with splayed legs, I had seen little, but the sounds remained in my head and later I would recall them during a televised women's tennis match, from random songs, the pneumatic hiss of a lowering bus, and at my Whitby school in the purring laughter of a group of Caribbean students who had recently transferred from Scarborough. I noticed them glancing at me from time to time in the lunchroom, but I felt no connection with their jovial, boisterous manner. This was odd because I had spent almost a third of my life in Trinidad. Maybe I had listened too long to my father's tirades.

I avoided him even more after that episode, but I don't think he noticed. Sometimes, after band practice, I walked down to the lake, about an hour away. Frequently, I slept in. The band soon separated, but I kept up my friendship with Liberty, one of the members, not because she sang as if there was no tomorrow or because she smelled like peaches and gum or even because she was the first girl I had seen naked. It was because she hated her parents and the place from which they had emigrated. In her overcrowded room, while we smoked weed and drew on each other's bodies with our fingers, she said Liberty was not some crazy hippie name but was common among Romani refugees.

When we were caught shoplifting smokes, I enquired about her parents' reaction following the cops' visit and she shrugged her bare shoulders as if it didn't matter. She posed the same question to me, and I revealed that my father said why the hell I didn't get out of his place and go to my mother. It was not the first time either.

"And?" Whenever she looked up at me, her eyes appeared round and vulnerable. I told her when I moved out it would not be to family. We made love that night on her bed next to a masked buccaneer and a bear with one of its marble eyes hanging out and she was unexpectedly tender, holding me close as if it was the last time we would see each other.

She got a job for me at a pet shop, *My Family and Other Reptiles.* During her visits to the shop, she paid more attention to the owner, a thin lanky man who looked like a bubbled-out tube, and I soon realized she was sleeping with him even though he was maybe ten years older than her. It was okay, though, because I enjoyed being in the shop and caring for the reptiles with their fixed contemplative gazes. She dropped out in Grade 12 and during our last conversation in the pet shop, she told me she was moving away and was finally free of her family. "We should keep in touch," she said. "The world is not as big as we think." She traced her fingers along my shoulder and onto a lizard's aquarium on her way out and the reptile seemed to loosen from its membrane, like one of those sci-fi alien movies. "Time to split." It was another year before I could do the same.

I had not thought about Liberty for a while, and some of my old concerns resurfaced. My father replied to my call the next day. He thanked me for my message and said he had had a quiet birthday. His voice sounded hollow, like a lecture in an empty classroom. He mentioned Whitby was changing and I should come and see for myself. Did he remember how often he had asked me to leave his place? There was a long pause before I heard the receiver click.

He repeated the invitation the following year, but this time it was more urgent as if there were terrific things I should view before they were torn down and gone forever.

That Christmas holiday, my sister returned from Belgium, where she had spent a month after her ESL stint in South Korea. At The Ice Biscuit, she gushed about her time in South Korea, her school near the fortified fence, the temples—a surprise to me—and the journeys to Bali and Japan. It seemed a series of improbable adventures and romance: a scooter malfunction and a friendship with the mechanic, also a monk; a week with another teacher, from Algeria, sailing somewhere or the other. She formed relationships wherever she went and I jokingly asked if she was imitating Carmen Santiago, one of her childhood idols.

"You remember. Do you know after we left Whitby, mom repurposed one of her red jackets into a trench coat for me? I wore it all the time, pretending." She glanced at her vibrating phone. "Hey, why don't we visit dad now? It's Christmas in three days."

"You know how he reacts to surprises."

"Oh, c'mon, man. It will be just for a while. And we can take him presents."

"I didn't get him anything."

She rolled her eyes and got up. "It's not too late. We will buy him something now."

Reluctantly I followed her, trying to understand her frenetic energy. In her rented car, on the way to Whitby, a pair of pyjamas and sandals gift-wrapped in the back seat, I asked her, "What if he is not at home?"

"You mean if he has gone feteing with all the other youngsters?" She changed lanes swiftly and sped up. "Stop groaning. It's only half an hour's drive. And we could cut it in a good half if you want, youngboy."

"Bad accent," I told her. "Not even Trinidadian." As we approached Ajax, I wondered if she knew of our father's friendship with the teacher. Perhaps he was out with her and her children, if she had any. "Did mom have a boyfriend?"

She was looking at her GPS, and she shot me a glance. "Where did that come from?"

"Just wondering."

"Well, wonder no more. She was a catch, you know. Before cancer."

We said nothing to each other until we pulled into our father's driveway.

We stayed for half an hour at most. On our way back, my sister said, "Dad seemed happy to see us. We must do this more often."

"Why do you think he was happy?"

"Because his face lit up when he opened the door. And didn't you notice how sad he was when you insisted you had to leave early because you were working overtime for the holidays?"

"Yeah. For time and a half."

"So it's true then."

"Why would I lie?"

"I dunno. Maybe because you seemed ready to bolt the minute we got there."

"I think I know our father better than you do."

She drove in silence, gazing out at the Christmas decorations on the malls alongside the 401. Then she told me in a more familiar tone, "Stop sulking. When was the last time we three were together?"

"For mom's funeral."

"Exactly. Not all reunions are cause for mourning."

"Yeah." What I wanted to say was that she had no idea what I had to put up with. After a while, I asked her, "Do you miss mom?"

"Course I do. Especially at nights like these." She described their final Christmas and the gift she received, a toy box stuffed with photos of us when we were both young and a notebook with her favourite recipes and a sweater she had knitted and on which she had sewn, Go Brave. "She prepared me . . . "

Three weeks later, she texted me that she was at the airport on her way to Japan for another ESL stint. There were a few incomprehensible emojis and a follow-up text: Don't forget our last conversation. I couldn't understand if this was a reference to our mother's affirmative advice or my attitude to our father.

She was in Japan when our father had his first health issue. It was three days before I got hold of her. She asked if she should return and I explained his coronary angiogram was a minimally invasive day procedure, according to the surgeon. I didn't mention that when I was leaving, my father, wrapped in a blanket on his sofa, had enquired if I couldn't prolong my stay, and I truthfully explained it had taken me an hour and forty minutes to get home. Bus, streetcar, GO train, and another bus. "I want you to have this." At the door, I saw his hand snaking beneath the blanket to retrieve an envelope. "It's not much."

"I'm good," I told him and walked away. I believe it was the first time I felt guilty about anything connected with my father; the sight of him crumpled on the sofa, dark rings beneath his eyes, his thinning hair a mess, and grey stubble on his face remained with me. I decided I would call more frequently, and he always answered immediately, as if he were waiting by the phone. My sister seemed happy with this increased communication and one night, while we were messaging, she started talking about the traditions of ancestral respect and obligations in Japan.

When I visited my father next, my story had just been published. I took the magazine with me. He looked healthier and when I gave him the magazine, he began rummaging around the kitchen and living room for his glasses. He asked me to read it to him and I said it was long. He patted the sofa next to him. Reluctantly, I began.

"Winter is a time for uncorking memories of places that have slipped out of view. But I had no stored memories of the places passing by. Coldwater. Parry Sound. Estaire. I saw only quiet disappearances. A blank slate where there should have been joy."

I glanced at him and noticed the familiar look of disapproval, and suddenly the story no longer seemed special. I continued reading, quickly now. When I was finished, I saw the twist of his lips and waited for the criticism. "You know, when I arrived alone in Canada, those two months while I was waiting for you all . . . during those two months, my eyes were drawn to all the differences from back home. The way everything was arranged here. The laws and regulations. How people kept to themselves. Everything running on time." He raised his hand slowly to his lips like a smoker's reflex and wiped his mouth with the back of his palm. It was the gesture of an old man. "And then I began to look for everything familiar."

"After we arrived?"

"It took time."

I remembered the protracted silences when we were all living together in the Whitby high-rise. Parents standing next to each other in the kitchen, sitting at the table, in front of the small television bought at a garage sale, not saying a word to each other. At times I believed they were falling in the way of Canadians, quiet but watchful. There had been no arguments, no fighting, no accusations. The divorce had been a complete shock to me. But the corrosive vigilance remained. I saw my father as a watchman rather than as a parent. He always carried around a wary look pinched into his slim face, his jaw set, and his nostrils seeming to tremble as if he was sniffing out danger or defiance.

"I have to leave now," I told him.

He nodded and walked me to the door. "Can I keep this magazine?"

"Yeah, I have others."

"Is the story based on an actual visit?"

I saw the bus approaching and shouted while hurrying to the stop, "I made it up."

On the trip back to my place, I recalled Liberty's invitation to the farm, her new home, and my journey there. It had been the end of fall and everything appeared shattered, the bare trees, the rocks and the jagged outcroppings, the smokestacks, the dead lake. When I saw Liberty at the station, she, too, appeared lifeless. She had gained weight and walked with a slouch. In her pickup, she told me she was pregnant with their second child. During dinner, she constantly got up to see about a screaming toddler, and her husband—who I had assumed was the lanky pet store owner but was actually a big man with a moustache that remained motionless as he slowly chewed his food—didn't speak a word to me.

When she was dropping me at the terminal, I asked why she had invited me and she said she wanted to see someone from her past. "Just to make sure I didn't imagine it." Was I still with my father? I replied that I had moved out and was working as a tour guide.

"Seeing anyone?"

"Off and on."

"One of those." She turned her head to look outside at two men in denim jackets loitering outside a convenience shop, so I couldn't gauge her meaning. I wanted to ask if she regretted marrying so young, but I guessed she was not running away from family, as I had thought when we were together, but trying to find one. Just before the bus terminal, she asked me, "Do you remember you once told me that people like us were like snakes shedding our skin and becoming humans?"

"Yeah. In your room." It was our first intimate moment and she had revealed the scar beneath her bangles. We avoided talking about our parents but she said that night that our parents were too consumed by their own struggles to understand that ours were more difficult because we never had the time to grow scales. That statement remained with me and soon after that visit, I started my story. For months, I never got beyond the first paragraph until one night I began once more, omitting the names of people and places. Maybe I wanted to hold the world at a distance.

My father's second stroke was more alarming than the previous and my sister arrived from her ESL job with a slim Japanese boy who was constantly raking back his fringe. He had an impish half-smile and I couldn't determine if he understood the surgeon telling my sister our father had a Transient Ischemic Attack or a ministroke which frequently resolved on their own. He was released the following evening from the Oshawa Hospital and my sister and her companion accompanied him to his place. She called daily with an update. A week after her arrival, she revealed that she had to return soon to her job. I should move in with our father, she said.

I had my first quarrel with her then, but I eventually agreed because it was the only practical solution. She would have done the same for our mother if the situation were reversed. I expected I would stay with him until he got better, maybe a couple of weeks at the most, but I ended up staying much longer. Apart from a minor tremor in his left hand, he seemed the same. Physically, anyway. He forgot some of our brief conversations from the previous mornings and once I saw him looking for the glasses pushed onto his forehead. I would have assumed that these were acts designed to make me prolong my stay, but some of his old irritability returned. However, his annoyance was different, not directed at me but to the caregiver, an amiable woman from the Philippines who came once a week to assist him.

While I was arranging with Beck Taxi to get the night shift, explaining that my father was ill, I wondered why I was doing this. I would save some rent money but not much, because of the additional travelling. I wondered what my children, if I had any, would make of this period in my life if I recounted it. It seemed a backward step for me to take. As the months passed, I felt an undefined feeling towards my father, different from the resentment of previous years. It was uneven and unpredictable and generated from minor issues. One late evening as I was leaving for work, he said, “People who talk about clean breaks don’t know what they are talking about.” It sounded like a challenge and I walked away. Another day he said that people who forget small things forget everything.

My responses were noncommittal, "Yeah," or "That's good," before I hurried away. I am glad I held my tongue because it turned out that these reproachful utterances were not directed at me at all. Once I saw him at the table with a shoebox. He seemed confused, so I asked if everything was okay. He nodded, and I left for work. When I returned in the early morning, the shoebox was on the table. Inside, I found clippings of Trinidad. I expected the articles to be in line with his criticisms of the island, how life over there had degenerated, but they all described festivities like *J'ouvert* and *ramleela*. Some were accompanied by photographs of "river limes" and street vendors and a teahouse on a mountain, run by monks.

I assumed this was pure nostalgia, but a month later, he told me he didn't want to die in a place where snow would fall on his grave. The gravity of the statement seemed curious, and I asked if he was thinking of moving to BC. He thought for a while, then said, "Do you know that the distance from Whitby to Vancouver is the same as to Trinidad?"

My sister found all of this funny. She joked, saying it was good he was getting adventurous in his old age. The gaps between her responses to my messages lengthened with each passing month, and I supposed she was busy with her classes. I felt it was unfair that only I had to put up with my father in Whitby, but I also knew that she would reveal no hardships of her own. She was in a foreign country while I was in a familiar place. I wondered how this would all play out. My father was approaching seventy, the point where a long-term care facility would be the best option.

I was on the GO train when my sister called to say her stay in Japan would be longer than she had imagined. I gathered that the relationship with the fringed boy was serious. Perhaps she was awaiting some comment and during my silence, she said, "Ardently do today what must be done. Who knows? Tomorrow, death comes." She said it was a Buddhist saying she had seen on a temple wall, then added, "We are looking for a house in Okinawa."

One night, out of the blue, my father asked if I remembered his brother Rudy, a jovial man whose stammer rendered him incomprehensible whenever he was drunk. In my memory, his long hair was always gathered in a ponytail and his dark face and furtive eyes never matched what he was saying. He usually brought along fruits like balata and cherries he claimed grew only in the dense forests. I recalled my father calling him a rumshop Romeo, someone perpetually drunk and promiscuous. So I replied to the question with a shrug.

At that my father got up from the table and stood before the bedroom door, blocking my path. He said that Rudy, who had been living in our old split-level flat, was moving to his daughter's place. "To be close to his grandchildren in the town." I thought this particular regret was the purpose of the conversation. It was a month before he revealed the real reason: his brother had agreed to sell the property to him. "I am planning to move there before the year is over," he said as if it were nearby, in Ajax or Oshawa. I told him this was a big move, and he surprised me by using a phrase from my story. He said he just wanted "a quiet disappearance."

I texted my sister that morning and when I awoke for work, I saw her reply, "Wow. That's great." I wanted to ask if she was crazy. A seventy-year-old man who had had a stroke, minor though it was, moving to a place rampant with lawlessness. I called her after work and asked if she recalled all his criticisms about the island. "That was just to convince himself he had made the right choice. When things didn't work out, it was easier to blame the island." I was about to remark that she saw everything through her rose-tinted glasses, when she added, "Mom's words."

"Did she say that?"

"Yeah. She also said that he was always harping on every type of people, except indigenous groups outsmarted and betrayed because they had no idea of dishonesty. You should have talked to her more often. Sorry, man, I didn't mean that."

"It's okay."

"She would have supported the move. Do you know what she told me once? That dad was the one pushing to leave the island but once we got here . . . well, you know the rest." Not as much as you, I wanted to say. "We should encourage him."

"Yeah."

I heard her laughing over the phone. "That's all you ever say. Have to run now, big brother. Talk later."

I couldn't take my sister's advice. I tried to engage my father, understand his reasoning, dissuade him. I printed online articles that referenced crime and abandoned hospitals. He read silently, lightly dusting the pages every few seconds, and I wasn't sure if the dispiritedness on his face was an acknowledgment of what he was reading or because I was not supporting his move. One morning, he told me, "I thought about India but it's too far away."

India! I remembered his condemnation of the country in the past. Then, as now, he was reading a newspaper article. That earlier article was about a poll. "Do you know why all these polls that investigate racism among minorities conclude that Indians as barely affected? It's because these people never see abuse as discrimination. It's deserved somehow." I would have forgotten that outburst if he had not turned it on me. I remember him glancing at my patched jeans and the guitar slung on my shoulder. "And you will do the same thing if they ask you these questions. You and everyone else."

I left him alone with his plans, but the next day, he revealed that he was "finalizing a few bank issues" and would leave at the end of the month. I called my sister immediately, and she texted me later to say she already knew. I wondered if he had also revealed all of this to his Filipino caregiver, but my slight offence was soon displaced by worry. Over the following days, I presented him with even more extreme articles—pensioners murdered, expatriates violently robbed, police corruption. I read him an article that mentioned the island was becoming a trans-shipment point for cocaine. He listened attentively and asked, "Why are you telling me this?"

"Because I don't want you to be murdered."

"I know the place. I will be safe."

"Maybe it's changed."

"And so have I." He got up. "*You* never liked change."

"This is not about me."

"Exactly." I saw him in the kitchen pouring water from a jug, and his face, for just a moment, looked exactly as when he was condemning my taste in music, my choice of clothes, my friendship with Liberty. And at that moment, I felt like telling him he was responsible for my moodiness that my sister joked about. He had never prepared me for anything. Later, in my room, I realized how childish this was and resolved that since he was intent on leaving, our last conversation would be amicable.

I didn't get the opportunity. The next morning, when I returned from work, I saw three envelopes spread on the kitchen table. One contained receipts for taxes and utilities that he had prepaid for a year, the other a deed with my name on it for the Whitby property, and the third all the articles I had presented him with.

It's now a month since he left and I have not spoken to him since. The week of his departure, I went into his room and rummaged through his bookcase and closet, looking for a number or some contact information. At the bottom of his closet, pushed behind an assortment of ties, I saw an old cigar box. On the lid was a Trinidadian phone number and when I called, I heard a voice, unrecognizable if not for the stammer. I identified myself and said I was trying to get in contact with my father. I heard him saying "the old b-boy" was in the village and was doing well. He had been attempting to restore phone and internet service, but it was taking time. According to Rudy, the old boy didn't mind because it was peaceful. "H-he taking a lil las' lap." He explained the term denoted a last hurrah.

When I hung up, I opened the box and saw an assortment of old photographs. One seemed to be on a university campus with my father lounging on a bench. The other was at a beach. His hair was long and his hands were in the air. He was dancing with the ocean in the backdrop.

Broken Pieces

It was a time in my life when I was not troubled by the notion that we might present ourselves to watchful strangers as occasional lovers sniffing out our differences. Our only common trait was our humour and even that was different. Mine was dark and squinty and Emily's was, at first, light and limber. One could say that it mimicked our appearances.

We met twenty-five years ago in a small rundown coffee shop inhabited mostly by retired workers from the GM plant in Oshawa, men in their seventies with baseball caps and grimaces etched into their faces even while perusing the *Toronto Sun*. The coffee shop was a place of readers. The high-school girls who worked evening and night shifts always had their texts, and I was still lugging around my Gutiérrez and Castellanos novels. Her interest lay in an odd combination of sci-fi paperbacks and glossy self-help books.

It was the latter that started our friendship. During a frigid January evening, I asked her, "Is the book helpful?" She was reading *How to Regulate Your Addictions*, and I was trying to quit cigarettes. She tipped back her parka and shrugged. I would have left it there, but she drew closer and leaned against the wall. The no-smoking bylaw had just come into effect and her hand holding the cigarette was shivering.

"Mine is smoking," I said.

"Oh, I thought it was like, you know, Charlie Sheen's issues."

It took a while before I understood and I told her, "Nah. No chance of that."

"No opportunities then?"

I wanted to make myself safe by mentioning a woman a thousand miles away, but she was disinterestedly blowing smoke rings, so I said lightheartedly. "Everyone is entitled to one addiction. What's yours?"

"Depends on who I am fucking?"

"Your mother know you talk like that?" Slipping into an ambiguous accent usually elicited a better response than speechlessness.

"She taught me everything. Craziness most of all."

"I haven't seen you here before. Where are you from?"

"Everywhere. And where y' longs to?" she asked, grinning.

When I understood, I told her, "Nowhere."

"You look like a pusher."

"And you, a stripper. Maybe we should barter."

She made a face and returned inside.

The next evening, she came to my table. She was wearing cargo pants and a camouflage coat that emitted a faint aroma of marijuana. She sat and withdrew two pill bottles, which she placed between us. She squinted and switched the bottles. "Decisions."

After a few minutes of watching her exchange bottles, I asked, "Red pill or blue?"

She caught on and said, "Think I will take both. I like to exist on all planes."

At the time I thought Emily was joking, but her mood swings were sudden and unpredictable. This instability was, at first, a complication in our friendship and later, its glue. We became chatmates because we were the only regular customers under forty. There was an occasional visitor our age, a lanky, shabbily dressed man who often glanced in our direction while waiting for his order. She remarked, without explaining, that he exuded "narc vibes" and I wondered about her experiences with the law. I didn't ask because some things she was tight with. For instance, she spoke affectionately of a pet dog but little of her parents. (Her description of the theft of both her dog and her boyfriend by "a larded-up bitch" had a burlesque feel that I didn't know what to make of.)

There was this one time, though, when she revealed that her family had moved from place to place, always renting because of her father's paranoia about the roof suddenly caving in. Eventually her mother got fed up and took her back, when she was eleven, to her grandparents. Her father disappeared and for a long time she had this dream that he was trapped in a toppled-down house in some remote ramshackle town. Each morning she saw her grandfather at the window with a toothbrush dangling from his mouth, shooting at the snapping turtles in the backyard pond. Her grandmother had a room filled with porcelain dolls and stuffed animals—her pets, she called them. Years later, when the old woman forgot her family's names, she remembered those given to her dolls. "It's sad, the way people fade away. Better they go all at once. The ones they leave behind can get it faster out of their system too."

I was able to determine that she had dropped out of college to follow a man to the west coast, and when that relationship ended, she moved across the country, returning home briefly at the death of her grandparents. There, she renewed her hostility toward her mother. It was like listening to someone from another world. Of job offers and gentle chiding from the cops and help from strangers and fruitful therapy sessions and the confidence to travel without provocation. I had moved to Canada four years earlier, but she was describing a place I did not know. Sometimes, following our conversations, I wondered if I had unconsciously drawn a three-mile radius into which I had garrisoned myself. Job at the grocery on one end, coffee shop on the other. And my novels to stave off my occasional homesickness.

A couple of weeks after we first met, she asked jokingly if the characters in my novels were grocery attendants. I was reading the *Dirty Havana Trilogy* by Gutiérrez at the time and when I described the roguish main character, she licked her lips and said she would like to meet the character one day in a coffee shop like this one. Sometimes, it was hard to know whether she was being arch or serious. Another evening, I came with my stained grocery pullover. She told me she always liked a man in uniform. That same evening, she mentioned she felt like murdering an occasional customer, a lanky, flu-afflicted man who had the maniacal and steadfast gaze of a beekeeper. "I hate nose sounds. Sniffles. Grunts. Deep breathing."

"Wet lapping sounds for me."

"Guess we will never hook up then."

"Guess not."

"Then you should stop leering at me." She pouted and adopted the breathy, sultry voice of an old-time actress, "Undressing me with your eyes."

"You should be more worried about all these old men here, Lucille Ball."

She glanced around. "Horny bastards. Do you think they still have wives at home?" She got serious and tapped her long fingers on the table. Her nails were all chewed down. "I had a fling with an old guy once. He was forty and married."

"That's not all that old."

"Eight years ago, it was. I was twenty-three, in college, and needed the money. I guess I felt a bit of love too."

"Were you happy?"

She shook her head and I asked, "Which is more important?"

"Happiness or love?" She got silent and looked away as if she wanted to leave it there. Eventually she said, "I wonder how many of these girls working here will take the money."

"They look too innocent."

"Sure they do." She shifted her gaze to me. "How about me? I have been told I have that abandoned cat look." She seemed both amused and serious. "How would you describe me? Lay it on me." She leaned forward and cupped her chin.

Because of the light-hearted tone of our conversation, I told her, "Your eyes are too close together. It makes your nose longer and your lips thinner." In truth, she was attractive in a bad-girl kind of way.

She laughed suddenly, harshly, drawing the attention of the other customers. "And you look like Ray Liotta's ugly brother."

She was still grinning, but she said it with such force I smelled her tobacco and mint breath. "I've heard worse," I managed to say. The following day, she looked at a mother walking across the road with her child and she wondered how our child, if we had one, would look. I told her, "Ugly, for sure."

She thought for a while. "I have a thing for ugly men. And women. I like little deformities. They add character." I tried to think of something clever to say but came up blank. "I think I inherited that from my grandfather. Lotsa crazies in these small towns."

"I have never been out of the city."

"That's a good thing. Your kind wouldn't be welcome there." She said this in a southern drawl, making it seem funny. She laughed awkwardly and changed the topic, but later when we were about to leave, she told me, "Even I wasn't welcome when I returned to the fold. I had broken the pact."

Sometimes I feel that true knowledge only comes from backward glances. At that time in my life, over twenty years ago, before the onset of cynicism from living in a country that forever withheld pieces of itself, my life was relatively uncomplicated. I judged people based on their friendliness and I assumed they did the same with me. I cannot say if it was wilful blindness, naivety, or the messy confidence young people sometimes possess that blinded me. It's not that I was not curious; for instance, I was drawn to the little tidbits Emily dropped about life beyond my bubble.

I never spoke much about myself and I parried most of her questions. Once she asked why I was always taking notes in my spiral notebook, and I lied about composing letters. She thought it may have been a diary and added, "I kept a diary in high school. When I realized my mother was secretly reading it, I made up all kinds of weirdness. Drove her crazy, but I like to think it put a little spark in her boring life. Took a while before I realized my entries were fantasies, not inventions."

"She sounds like a normal mom."

"Reading my diary? All her moods were extreme. One morning, she came into the washroom and screamed for the entire town to hear, 'Is that a snake on your pussy?' It seems funny now, but it wasn't then. You don't believe me?" She was sitting opposite me and she slid down on her chair and unzipped her jeans. She was not wearing underwear and I could see the tattoo of a serpent's head, its forked tongue lost in the triangle of cropped light hair. I was about to jokingly ask if I could pat it but when I glanced around, I noticed one of the other customers, an old man with thick horn-rimmed glasses staring bleakly above his paper.

"You are drawing attention," I whispered. "Zip up."

She seemed annoyed with my request and for the rest of the night, she read her book. The next day she was her usual fooling-around self. During our smoke break, she asked me, "Have you ever thought about how you would like to go?" When I shrugged, she continued, "I would like to die peacefully in my sleep like my grandfather. Not like the screaming passengers in his taxi." Because of her lugubrious delivery, I was momentarily confused until she added, "It's an old joke. Seriously, though, I would like some say in how I go." During this time, perhaps because of familiarity, she began rolling her joints and puffing a few times before pinching them out. "Don't fucking look at me like that," she told me once. "It keeps me mellow."

"Guess it hasn't kicked in as yet."

Emily had a birdlike way of watching whenever she was undecided about anything—her head slightly inclined, not directly facing me, yet alert, as if waiting for my move. After a few minutes, she returned inside. This unpredictability became the pattern for the next couple of weeks. At first, I chalked it up to her personality, but I later assumed it was connected to her medication and marijuana. During a week of irritability, she revealed that her landlord had complained about the odour seeping into the adjacent apartment, newly occupied by an Arab couple and their baby. No one complains in my building, I told her. Somehow, that turned into an invitation and during the fifteen-minute walk, the icy wind rustling through the bare shrubs, she held my hand as if she might blow away. The last visitor had been almost a year earlier, a woman who worked briefly in the fish section at the grocery, but this one was different. We were like friendly sparring partners.

I blame my high for what followed; the last time I had smoked weed was during my university years. My memory of our act is not precise. Sometimes I think this is intentional. I remember us smoking the first joint on the sofa. The second on the floor. The smoke alarm in the apartment went off, and we somehow found it funny. Eventually, I stood on a stool, she holding onto my waist and supporting me as I removed the battery. "Cork your ears," she said.

Afterward, we lay on the ground and I told her, "I didn't see that coming."

"Me too."

We made proper love on the floor and, in my hazy memory, she opened herself, becoming uncharacteristically tender and vulnerable. She asked if I had a regular girlfriend and I told her I had been engaged to a woman who could never get a visa and who had finally tired of waiting. She said it was sad to be forever waiting. Better the bad news come all at once. I couldn't tell if her sympathy was for my ex-fiancée or myself or someone else. She had been in a dozen relationships and concluded that men were all users. I mentioned my more limited experience with women I described as crazy. She eased up, resting on the crook of her elbow, and looked at me for a while with an expression I could not decipher. Then she lay down once more, her cheek against my shoulder, and exhaled loudly. I thought she had fallen asleep, but she began to talk slowly and with long pauses about her mother's attempts at suicide when they returned to her grandparents' place. During her last visit there, she got into an argument with a neighbour who was always hurling abuses at her mother over the fence. She brought out her grandfather's old shotgun and sat on the porch whenever the neighbour returned from work. For the first time, she spoke of her mother sympathetically. "If I had remained there, I wouldn't have known what women have to put up with. It seemed normal." In spite of this, she had recently thought of returning. "What about you?" she asked.

I told her for two months following my arrival, my suitcases were not fully unpacked because of my uncertainty. But I couldn't return. I had given up too much to move here and it would be difficult to reassemble the pieces. She wondered why people went through the trouble of leaving all the familiarity behind and starting new lives. In the end, it's all the same, she said. A warm droplet trickled onto my shoulder and I realized she was crying.

I was unnerved by this new side to Emily and I felt strangely embarrassed the next day on my way to the coffee shop. I didn't know how we could resume our harmless flirtation. She was not there, and I guessed she felt the same way. That entire week, she did not turn up, and I noticed the regulars glancing at me from time to time. Somehow, they seemed more relaxed and I couldn't say whether it was because they were disapproving of our friendship or of the presence of a rebellious-looking woman in camouflage coats and cargo pants.

A week later, she turned up in a grey business suit. She ordered a coffee and told me she had returned from a job interview. She didn't get the job but over that month I got used to her new attire as she went to other interviews. Her visits were now brief, and she never mentioned our night together. Then one evening she stayed until closing. She asked if I would walk with her to the bus stop. It was a nippy mid-spring night and we sat on a bench just before the stop. She leaned onto my shoulder and slipped her hand into my coat pocket. The bus came and went. From her breathing and the way her hand was clenching and unclenching the inner lining of my coat I felt she wanted to say something. I assumed it was about our night together but she told me her father had died. She had got the news about a month earlier. She had never spoken of her father before, other than his fear of roofs. She couldn't remember much but she described his slicked-back hair and goatee and fondness for lobster. During her last visit to her mother, she found a trove of letters from him hidden in the closet. He had remarried, which came as a surprise to her.

Another bus came and went. I asked if she was okay now and she said it was like grieving twice. Abandonment, and death.

I realized that her behaviour during the last month or so was because she had been wrestling with the news. "Remember when you told me it's too late to pick up the pieces or something? Maybe . . . but sometimes it's good enough just to see where they landed." I didn't understand what she meant until she revealed that she was returning to the house her grandparents had built. The house in which her mother still lived. Emily's last words to me were, "I am going to see what I missed."

That was twenty-five years ago, on this very spot, and I remember the stark look on her face, her hands fumbling in my coat, the tremor in her voice, as though it were yesterday. I folded the newspaper containing the article of the small-town nurse who, besieged by the deaths she was witnessing daily, decided she'd had enough. I watched the buses passing by for a while before I got up and walked to the old coffee shop, now gone.

The Pen Pal

One evening, while he was walking along the deserted Lakeshore, his foot swept a robin. It was the end of fall when everything seemed eviscerated. Colours, odours, motion, texture. November, this indifferent month, was his favourite and during his recent strolls, his attention always on the ground before him, he sometimes recalled an article from a science journal that explained how our view of the past deepened as we expanded our gaze. The writer was referring to the universe, but he had been drawn to this notion of keeping the world at a distance by never looking back.

He stood for a while, not sure what he was expecting or what he should do, and when he noticed the bird's feet twitching, he hurried on, thinking it would be better if he had stepped on the weak body and ended its misery. Insects were already about, drawn to the scent of death and soon they would swarm the dying bird.

These evening walks, especially after the stresses of his classes, were always calming but now his thoughts drifted once more to the cream envelope, sealed with a sticker of spiralling roses, that he had retrieved from his mailbox the previous day. Inside was a folded sheet of parchment paper. The hurried writing and the uneven wavy letters did not match the formality and the substance of the contents.

It had begun with a challenge and an apology.

"You may not remember me, likely because we have never met. Perhaps we were passing acquaintances. But what really is a passing acquaintance? All acquaintances are passing; if not, they soon become clawing (hah!) and dyspnoeic." The sender, who signed off with the name Grace, was from South Carolina, a state he had never visited and about which he knew little. He had placed the letter in his briefcase and during the morning recess at his college he reread it. The writer's breast cancer had metastasized to her bones, lungs, and liver and her doctor had advised her to make peace with the world. So she had posted copies to everyone with whom she had come into contact. Because of her profession, the list, compiled from several address books and email contacts, was extensive and disorganized. At the end of the page, she apologized if the letter had been sent to someone unacquainted.

The following morning he spotted a young couple embracing beneath a tree and he wondered if the letter-writer was a university fling from a quarter century earlier. He quickly dismissed this notion, as there had been the suggestion of a sinewy humour he could not recall in his former partners.

Later in the day, while his class was reading *Tess of the D'Urbervilles*, he thought of the letter. He guessed this was because of the harsh hand the two women, the heroine of the novel and his letter-writer, had been dealt. The letter, though, could not be more different from Hardy's fatalistic tone, and its composer, until her last diagnosis, seemed in control of her life. Other tragic characters too brought this woman to mind. Lena Grove. Rosa Dartle. Juliet and Ophelia. Helen and Hera. All the women in the nineteenth-century American lit course.

A week passed and he was reminded daily of Grace. This was

disconcerting because, after the turbulence of his breakup and relocation, he had streamlined his life into a narrow focus. The one activity he had not given up—and the only thing he looked forward to—was his hour-long solitary walk each evening. During that hour, he would feel the stresses of the day melting away: the departmental rivalries, the worthless conversations, the lumpy flirtations of middle-aged men and women.

Now, during his strolls, he could not put aside the letter. Not so much the disease it mentioned but rather its unusual tone and language. He tried to imagine the expression on the writer's face, the texture of her skin, the clothes she wore, the view outside her window, the clutter on her table, the colour of her walls, the leaves on her potted plant as she wrote phrases like "the deliquesce of delight" and "the furtiveness of errant joy" and "the withholding gaze." She preferred to not use bcc in her communications because she did not want to "instigate a community of mourners."

During his half-hour in the lunchroom, he glanced at the other teachers leaning forward on their cushions of fat as they bit into their gristle and dusted crumbs from their trousers. He listened to the whistling laughter that interrupted their chomping and he thought of the letter writer ravaged by the disease but ever graceful. (Once, he was shocked to imagine her as improved by cancer, with chiselled cheekbones and fragile eyes, mulling over her losses.)

Sometimes he overheard whispered conversations about Mel, a teacher in her mid-forties whose husband may or may not have left her following some traumatic event, and although the staff offered her sympathetic greetings in the corridors, he always kept his eyes on the ground whenever he passed her.

Life takes its course was his attitude, formed as he was bounced around as a boy. It had been his sister, fifteen years younger, who stood vigil over their mother's bed and who consented to the removal of the life support system. He had never been good with big decisions. That was a frequent accusation of his partner, who waited half their time together for him to make the first move. She described her affairs, countered his provocations with graphic details of her lovers, and all he could come up with was, "Fascinating. One day we must both write about this."

"How can you be so utterly dead?" she had retorted once. In the context, "utterly" was redundant, he told her. You are either dead or not. And when she slammed her door, he went to the study for his book, *A Tale for the Time Being* by Ruth Ozeki. After three weeks of blistering silence, he eventually moved out. He took his books and for months they remained in the boxes into which he had transported them. During drunken nights, he and whoever he had snagged in a club or bar, stumbled over the boxes on their way to his bed.

"You should get rid of these," a woman older than him by a decade had said one morning behind a puff of smoke. "Or else get a cat."

He couldn't understand the connection, but that week he bought a cheap plyboard bookcase. He spent the following days reordering his apartment, discarding the accumulated junk, and he was surprised by the calming effect of the process. And in that period of calm—he believed it would not last—he impulsively chucked his job at the library and applied to teachers' college.

The tranquillity did not leave him; instead, it transformed into sluggish neutrality, a disinterest that allowed him to bypass everything not related to his courses and, later, to his classes. With his food, his few interactions and his pastimes, he was satisfied with the bare minimum. He saw himself as a marginal man; marginal but content.

Grace's letter changed that. And as the days passed, so did his impression of the mystery writer. In the school library, he researched late-stage breast cancer and he imagined this woman not at her desk gazing with her contemplative eyes at the view outside the window but vomiting in her sink, foraging through her medicine cabinet, raging at her illness. Yet he was always brought back to the language of the letter. While he was teaching, he sometimes ranged through a list of her possible occupations. Teacher, researcher, librarian, writer. She had not mentioned a husband or children but he felt she was not a young woman. She was not old, either. "I shall hold my experiences close to my chest," she had written. "And let these rather than the sorrow of unlived years carry me to the end. I shall not reproach myself. If blame there must be, I will stamp it onto the disease I have given a name. The Masked Marauder."

In the beginning of December, one month after he opened the envelope, he was summoned to the principal's office. Parents' Day would be the following Tuesday, he heard the principal reminding him and it would be fantastic if he displayed some interest in their concerns. The principal went on to say that he was an otherwise diligent teacher, but he was pondering the word *fantastic*. Existing solely in fancy, he thought, and permitted himself a brief smile.

The principal's concern this year was misplaced; for the first time he was not bored by the excuses or irritated by the sly boasts of the parents. He focused on the mothers, studying each face, wondering if any of them was hiding a secret, a disease maybe that would soon become visible. He would lean forward on the table, clasp his hands beneath his chin, murmur, and cluck his tongue sympathetically. The mothers were duly alarmed, but he found himself unexpectedly moved by their recollections of minor distresses. Are you okay? A parent asked when he began to sniffle.

He recovered on his way home, but he knew he could not allow this to continue. He stopped at a stationery store and bought a sheaf of light-blue paper and a sympathy card with the words,

"May Time Heal your Sorrows." When he got home, he cast aside the card because the language felt too bland and canned. He spent half the night trying to frame the letter; attempting to imitate Grace's bleak humour, her nimble toss of words. In the end, he gave up and simply said he had received her letter more than a month earlier and could not determine if it had been sent in error. He expressed his sympathy and complimented her on her resilience.

The minute he dropped the envelope into the mailbox, amendments came to mind. He regretted its brevity and felt he should have mentioned a bit of himself and his job and perhaps included a stanza from Emily Dickinson, whose poems he had taught the last semester.

The ambivalence trailed him the following week, and he either considered he should have been more encouraging or maybe more formal. Perhaps he might have mentioned his phone number and email address, although Grace had included neither. Each evening he hurried to his mailbox, but he knew that unless she too replied by express delivery, her response would come in a week or more.

During his lunch break at school once, he researched facts about South Carolina and learned that it was frequently in the path of hurricanes and there had been some vote or the other about the Confederate flag flying on public buildings. He read of roaming wild hogs and movies like *Swamp Thing* that had been filmed there and of the quaint laws such as one banning the use of bathtubs for horses, and he worried for Grace even though he realized he was just cherry-picking bizarre facts. During a blustery winter night, while the wind rocked his windows, he imagined himself standing before her door with a suitcase at his side. The house he pictured was a plantation-style mansion, and she was wearing a diaphanous white gown.

That image, drawn most likely from an old film, was a ridiculous fantasy, and as the days passed and his mailbox offered the usual bills and flyers, he admitted that his obsession with Grace's letter, sent obviously in error, was simply silly. The poor woman had probably passed away by now. Then one day, he received a package. He recognized the handwriting immediately but resisted the temptation to open it in the elevator. In his study, he put it on his desk and went into the bathroom. He emerged ten minutes later, his hair damp and a towel around his waist. He glanced at the package while changing and poured himself a glass of port from a bottle he had had for years.

Finally, he sat at the desk and took a drink. The liquid was rippling in the glass. He put the glass aside and steadied his hands as he cut the tape and the twine. There were two pages from a three-ring notebook folded against each other with a clip and another sheet similar to the serrated cream paper he had received earlier. He began with the two pages; when he unfolded them he was astounded to discover they were in his writing; not in his present style of lightly joined block letters, but with a flourishing italicized script that curled at the end of each word. It had been an affectation of his middle-school years and he had maintained this style to the dismay of his teachers until he entered high school.

He began to read the first page.

Dear Gracie,

I saw your name in the pen pal section of the newspapers and decided to write because we have the same hobbies. I never knew girls liked comic books too. Most of the boys from school prefer superheroes from DC and Marvel but I enjoy Gold Key, Charlton, and Dell. My favourites are Tales from the Crypt and Vault of Horror and those describing multiverses. Frank Frazetta is my favourite artist.

The letter continued on this note, referencing comic books and their creators. He had forgotten about that phase in his life and he felt he had been showing off in his letter.

He unfolded the second letter. It exhibited more familiarity, and he asked about her cat—which she had lost for a night—and mentioned his own wish for a dog. That letter would have been written about the time his parents had separated, but there had been no mention of that. He remembered pleading with his mother, in whose custody he had remained, that a dog would keep him company when she had to work nights at the restaurant. She explained she could not afford a pet, and he turned his attention to his father, whom he visited during March break. His father had been drunk as usual and he recalled the clutter of his place and his regular fights with a woman who slept over. Both mocked him by pretending to whistle for a dog whenever he was around and doubling over with wheezing laughter.

He had imagined the pair wheezing, too, from the fire a few months later, which took both their lives. His mother betrayed no emotions or explanations, even when she moved to another town. Soon after, she was pregnant and when his sister was born, no one turned up to claim paternity. He never asked. At his new high school he was moody and studied in spurts, just enough to get through his courses. His moodiness followed him at his part-time job at the Little Photo Studio that was adjoined to a gas station. There he met a girl who was saving for university. He could not recall the exact moment he decided to do the same but he remembered when he revealed this to the girl. It was late in the night and they had just emerged from the darkroom. While she was buttoning her blouse, she asked when he planned to tell her.

After years of living with his increasingly dispirited mother, he had learned to avoid nuances and to speak literally, so he said that he had not planned on anything other than saving enough money for university. This took him a year longer than the girl, but they kept up a sporadic correspondence and when he entered university, he moved in with her.

He was surprised by these pleasant memories of the girl he would later marry. He recalled the nights he laid her, reeking of diesel, against the table on which were trays of chemicals. The owner of the studio had threatened to fire him for this, but he always said that no one else could spot minor distortions in the development of negatives. He was an expert at detecting anomalies.

He took the letters to the window and looked out. He was now forty-three, the entire lifetime of his father. When his mother was his age, she had already given up on life. But was he any different? At the window, with snow pattering lightly on the pane and clouding the trees, he reread both letters he had sent Grace almost three decades earlier, and he was astonished that he sounded like any other boy of thirteen or so. His memories had constructed another life entirely. Still at the window, he unfolded the cream page.

The tone of this letter from Grace was more upbeat than the last, and until he arrived at the last paragraph, he assumed there had been some improvement in her condition. But he read, "The disease is like one of those wicked stepmothers I used to dream about as a child; it has taken over my life completely. Alas! I am afraid there is no magic wand, no prince traipsing through the snow with a magical charm."

Once more, the unexpected playfulness!

That night he wrote her a letter three pages long. He had never experienced this fluency and upon rereading it seemed written by a stranger. He spoke of faith and the healing abilities of animals and the strength of the mind and recalibrating the brain. He didn't mail it because he suspected it was simply a variation of the fantasy-tinged letters he wrote to her as a boy.

In the morning, he concluded that he had been taking her references to magic wands and princes too literally and he mailed her a new, hurriedly composed letter in which he thanked her for including the pen pal letters and reminding him of a more joyous period in his life. He also exhorted her to keep faith and mentioned Mel, the fellow teacher who, he recently learned, had survived stage four cancer for close to five years.

He spoke as if he knew this teacher, but the truth was she had been mostly cordoned off by her little circle of sympathizers. But that week he sought her out, and when he met her alone in the corridor, he said hello and commented on the weather. She seemed surprised and did not answer, but during the lunch break, she separated from her group and came over to his table where he was sitting alone. "I'm in remission," she said. "I should have mentioned that earlier."

"That's good," he said awkwardly, before she walked away to rejoin her group. He was relieved their conversation had been brief but during his afternoon classes, he felt lighter than usual, as if the teacher's diagnosis had somehow been transferred to Grace.

He received her response a few days earlier this time. She thanked him for his letter and mentioned the oddness of receiving encouragement from a pen pal from whom she had not heard for close to three decades. "Perhaps the sound of distant cheering feels more unfeigned because it is not cluttered with obligations and wily reproaches." She added, possibly as an afterthought, that she had sequestered herself in a place where the only sounds were of the doldrums. It seemed a strange phrase, until he realized she had referred to the sound of the wind current.

In his response, he said he had been glad to help, and he briefly mentioned his conversation with Mel. He also said that doldrums could also describe his life, but he felt it was a necessary alternative to the chaos always around the corner. The minute he mailed it, the usual regret followed and he suspected she would not reply. But two weeks later, he received her response. It was more intimate, he thought. She had once worked with waves and her "coworkers were mostly blackcaps and bitterns." She missed the sound of the ocean, so she had moved closer to the beach once she realized her "disease was a steadily solidifying shadow." Her doctor had recommended she place herself on a list for an experimental treatment that harnessed the body's immune system, but she had tried so many therapies, had been so weakened by radiation and chemotherapy and splintered hopes that she was not up for anything else. She ended by saying, "But I should stop complaining. My life exceeded my expectations in every way but this. And I still have my waves."

In his subsequent letter, he remarked that fearful of repeating his parents' miserable experiences, he had tried to organize his life as best as he could. He revealed that for most of his adult life, he had been shifting between the behaviours of both his parents: the drunken excesses of his father and the dour fortitude of his mother; between chaos and stagnation.

This untypical revelation may have been an attempt to match her confessions, but it felt easy chatting with her. *Chatting*. He thought of the word for a while, a little taken aback by its intimacy. In her reply, she said she had been the same, not by choice but by disposition, and now she wished she could introduce some chaos into her life. "Not the kind that comes from wondering at the morning's reaction to my medication or tumbling in the ocean during a simple swim, but a funny, crazy, farcical topsy-turvyness, like a circus filled with wondrous and impossible feats. A balagan!"

Such were their letters: she reporting what she missed and he describing what he had blunted. One night, while he was describing his late-night liaisons with his ex in the darkroom over two decades earlier, he wondered if he was falling in love. He froze; and for a week he glanced at the letter on his desk, afraid to mail it.

In the nights now, he dreamed of her. He was standing on the shore and watching her wade into the ocean, her bitterns and herons cutting into the water. He was two rows behind her in a circus and observing her laugh and gasp as clowns walked the tightrope and trapeze artists and acrobats tripped and fell on their enormous feet and tigers bounced on trampolines. The following week, he carried his letter with him each morning, and when he returned at the end of the day he thought that it felt heavier; he ignored his mailbox. But on Friday, when he returned from school, he checked it and saw the familiar handwriting.

She hoped he had received her last letter. Perhaps email might be more convenient, but she had unplugged herself and only went online at the local library once a week. During her last visit there, she had read of a woman who had organized a "going out party," inviting her family and friends to her house. She had also itemized all her belongings, with notes on them saying who should get what. After an evening of wine and music—a sister playing the harp, a cousin the guitar, and her husband on the drums—she was wheeled out to the mountain that hung above her place, and there she took a doctor-prescribed dose of pentobarbital and chloral hydrate. "It's a lovely picture, but I do not have a mountain or musically inclined relatives. I can guess what you are thinking. But there is no shame in wanting to go, you know. To leave with no fuss. No backward glance, no worry about unfinished business. Just to disappear from this world. Quietly sneak away. Quietly, quietly, not like a whimper but a whisper."

He felt like crying. He knew he must offer a counter-narrative, but what could he say? That choosing one's end was reckless? There was always hope? That she should count the blessings of her allotted time on earth? Who was he to offer advice to a woman a thousand miles away, with a disease he knew little of, with a past he could not imagine and one she had never really described?

His letter began with lies. He wrote that he had not replied earlier because he had been away. He tore it up, started again, and said there was a mail strike. That, too, he discarded. He put on his jacket and went in the lake's direction. It was already dark, and the wind stung like slivers of glass against his face. As he passed the benches frozen to their spots overlooking the lake, he heard the faint screech of a gull and he imagined another bird he must have read about, a jungle crow. He felt a little thrill of fear, as if mad with hunger, it would fly towards him. He hurried along and picked up a sniffling chatter, some small animal at the root of a tree. So even in this cold and bereft place, there were signs of life. He just had to look for it. But his fear grew as he walked on the shore and, recalling the letters and remembering his *Tales from the Crypt* and other teenaged distractions, he considered that there was a malevolent quality to the stirrings of life where there should be none. Reanimated corpses and stalking ghosts. We have never outgrown this primitive dread of spirits, he thought.

He recalled his disgust when he first saw his mother with a tube sticking into her mouth and another snaking into her hospital gown. Her breathing was gasping and unnatural, her eyes oily in their slack pouches. He had cut back his visits and stopped visiting entirely in the month of her death. But considering his feelings now, walking into the dead night, trying to keep his disquiet at bay, he wondered if it had been fear rather than disgust. Life where there should be none. He felt that keeping someone on life support was one step from reanimating a corpse.

He slowed his steps. And he tried to create a continuum, linking all the events of his life that he had pushed aside. He recalled his seclusion in his tiny room following the visits to his father, the abrupt move to another town, the appearance of a baby, his mother's inertness broken only by the cries of his sister, or during a visit by one of the men who trooped into their jumbled apartment, the hurried cleaning before their visits and his refusal to help. He recalled his hatred spreading from his father to his mother, to his little sister, to everyone else, and to himself.

He thought of his later attempts to repair all that mess in his life and he felt he had learned to view his condition as representing not only disorder but also hiding a more twisted condition. Deformity.

Lights were twinkling on a little peninsula ahead and he realized he had walked further than he had done before. He turned to retrace his steps, and he wondered why the woman from South Carolina had not been a recipient, too, of his fear and disgust. Was it because she was too far away to affect his life? But hadn't she done so already? He thought of this on his way back. He strode faster, his fingers and ears freezing. Could it be the measures she had taken to prevent her distress from spilling onto others? And now, the consideration of leaving in a manner of her choosing and not burdening anyone.

He slowed a little as he approached the spot where he had heard the animal. The only sounds were crackling fractures from the trees and the icy ground. When he got to his apartment, he turned up the heat and sat at his desk. He opened his laptop and stared at the screen-saver's dissolving amber field with unravelling clouds for an hour before he began his letter. And when he was finished, he placed it into an envelope and walked out of his apartment. It was precisely two AM when he released the letter into the mailbox.

He rushed to the mailbox each evening and night. A week passed. He composed another letter. Life was precious, he wrote. Every last drop should be savoured. He scratched out "savoured" and replaced it with "cherished." He ended by saying that although he had never met her and had no idea of her appearance and would pass her straight by if their paths crossed, she had affected him more than anyone in recent memory.

Each day, he rushed from school. From his mailbox, he withdrew bills, flyers, and bank statements. Mid-week, he saw in the mailbox, his last letter to South Carolina, stamped with Return to Sender.

His mind moved from the crazy idea he should book a flight to South Carolina to the more assuring notion that if he were patient, he would discover a good reason for the undelivered mail. But this minor assurance did not last. He engaged in a variety of online name searches and followed links that led him to tragic accounts involving terminally ill children and prayers and donation sites. The world seemed to be rolled into a ball of suffering and despair and he could not understand the acceptance and the meagre hope of parents and siblings and spouses. Better to give up, he thought, than to have the tragedy stretched out for years and years. In the aftermath of these searches, he was grateful that he lived alone, unfettered, unburdened.

Yet gradually, this commonality of suffering seemed to shrink the world; there were so many tangential points of shared prayers and alternative therapies and accounts of survival and grief that Asia, Africa, and South Carolina appeared to possess no distance. One midday, he turned off his laptop and journeyed to the local library. The librarian explained that they did not stock copies of newspapers from South Carolina, but he could try the library's digitized site of the world's newspapers. And it was in a small local newspaper, *The Post and Courier*, that he found a single paragraph.

On his journey to his apartment, he felt weightless, and it appeared that the cars on the road, the few pedestrians, and the falling darkness had happened a while ago and he was viewing as an astronomer might view the outer reaches of the universe. The past is never gone, he thought. It's just further away. Memories, like viruses, ensure their survival by either clinging to or jettisoning data. On Monday, during the lunch break he walked across to

Mel's table. Her companions seemed a little startled because he had never spoken to the group but they all leaned in when he gave her the page he had photocopied in the library. They gazed at the picture of the woman, taken when she was in her late twenties, her hair blowing, her jeans rolled to her knees, the ocean behind her. "I have made my peace with the world." One of the teachers read Grace's final words and another looked up at him sympathetically.

He was about to say that he did not really know the subject of the article, when Mel said, not to him but to the group, "Sometimes we understand more of ourselves from the decision of others."

Later that evening, during his walk, he glanced up and saw a ripple of dark clouds ignited by the setting sun. As he continued along his regular route, he thought of his evening strolls as emblematic of his life. The confused intersection before the crowded lane leading to the quiet garden path, in the middle of which was a wooden bridge, icy in winter. Now he wished there was a secret trail, a path where the first step might shake off everything you thought you knew about yourself. An alternate universe, like in his old comic-book stories. He zipped up his coat and noticed that he was still wearing his old winter boots, bought a lifetime ago.

One and Another

She now spoke with prolonged pauses, her steely eyes fixed to a point, as if she was trying to determine the significance of some nearby object in her room painted a faint yellow in Redrose Manor. But occasionally, she began forcefully, catching him by surprise. Such a time was when she insisted he no longer visit because she had no memory of him. "I don't believe you," she said bleakly. "I have no idea who you are and why you are in my place."

He believed her, he truly did, for their affair had been a generation earlier, thirty-two years, to be precise and he, too, on his return journey, as he closed his eyes and listened to the carriage's metallic whine; he, too, was momentarily uncertain about how much was real.

He had been contacted by her daughter who, the last time he spotted her, was a confused child half-hidden in the darkness but on the appointed day in the café was nothing he expected. On the phone, her voice, formal to the extreme, was more reminiscent of a professor's languid delivery than a woman asking a favour of a man with whom her mother had had an affair. After the call, he reflected on whether the child's confused eyes had hardened into an adult's recriminatory stare. This had actually made his decision.

The café was filled with couples, and a few university students huddled over their laptops. He was looking for a woman who might bear some resemblance to her mother's wide-hipped voluptuousness, her unruly curls, and round amused eyes, but the figure that waved him over, bespectacled, erect in her seat, was tall and angular. She was built like her father, and had his air of casual disinterest. For some reason, that put him at ease.

After the formalities she began by asking about his family. He told her that his wife, whom he had divorced before meeting her mother, had passed away a few years earlier. He had never met his ex's son, born a year after the divorce, nor her grandchildren, but lately he wished there was some communication. He had been in a relationship for several years but now lived alone, comfortably, on a generous pension. He noticed her glancing around and realized she was not really interested in his life, so he asked how she had located him.

"My mother was meticulous in one regard," she told him. "Her diary." She must have noted his discomfort as he looked down to adjust the strap of his watch, for she added, "You are not the first person I contacted." He was surprised, though he should not have been, and he remained silent because anything he said might be construed as a belated judgment. "She gave a name to the diary. 'One and Another.' The entries, as I mentioned, were very precise, very detailed. I believe she may have been thinking of her diary as the framework for a novel, but for whatever reason, she changed her mind."

"I remember that phrase. One and another. She said it to me more than once." He observed her mild astonishment and did not bother to explain that it was one of those cute utterances that men and women in affairs invented to avoid other designations—like a clandestine affair or an adulterous couple—and so move the relationship into the realm of playfulness. Nor did he tell her, the daughter, that he had always assumed the phrase was used more personally, to refer to a single man and a solitary woman. What he asked instead was about the men she had contacted before him.

The daughter took a while to answer and he saw in her a trace of her father, who had usually been away at conferences, but during his appearances at the dinner table spoke with long, gentle pauses, weighing every word as if he were still in one of his classes, delivering a lecture. Now this man wished to speak through her to the father and reveal how he stumbled into the affair. He did not know where to begin.

"You are not under any obligation," he heard her saying. "It was a very long time ago. To answer your question, there were four men other than yourself mentioned in her diary. Two have passed away, one could not be located, and the other felt it necessary to defer. He needed to protect his family, I suppose." She got up and unclasped her purse. "This is the address. Redrose Manor." Before she walked away, she said, "In case you are wondering, my father also passed away."

He sat in the café for a while, observing the subtle smiles of the young women seated alone, as if a half-forgotten memory had interrupted their studious note-taking. The sharp angles on the face of the woman who had just departed his table made her appear stern and composed, and as he gathered his coat, he wondered how a daughter could be so dissimilar from a mother whose loose energy always ranged along the spectrum of amused recklessness. The latter's gestures and expressions had shifted so swiftly that he once imagined a runaway spasm bouncing around beneath her skin. Her favourite position had been astride him and sometimes before she shifted over, he would glance at her flushed face, the big round eyes, the parted lips, the slight overbite and be reminded of the women on campy Grindhouse movie posters.

All of which suggested he would meet a crazed old woman with fierce uncombed hair and unstable eyes at the Redrose Manor, which was lined along its path with crab apple and dogwood trees on the unusually windy fall afternoon of his visit. The wind had brushed the trees clean and bloodied the pathway. He felt like turning back, as if this splatter of red were a sign, but he had spent most of the morning choosing his outfit, discarding what he felt was too formal or too casual. He settled on a turtleneck sweater, grey trousers with a houndstooth pattern, and a trench coat. He imagined the neutral tone would provoke just the right amount of memory.

The woman, propped on the bed, watching his approach warily, was a complete stranger. She followed his movements as he placed the flowers on the coffee table and sat on a chair about six feet away. He began by asking her, "Is everything comfortable here?" and immediately felt the question was too proprietary, so he added, "The leaves outside are all red." It had been her favourite colour. To both utterances she remained unmoved, and he felt once more this burden imposed by the daughter. "You look good," he said.

She turned to the doorway, blinking slowly as if to dismiss him and his lie.

"We were friends once. For a year and a half. I came over when your husband was away at his conferences. I knew him too." It sounded like a defendant's evasive response to a badgering courtroom lawyer, but he didn't know what else to say. He looked at her profile, the dull eyes, the sagging eyelids, the downturned lips, the neatly combed iron-grey hair, and he felt that a generation ago her appearance had been directed by her vivacious personality, and with all of that gone now, there was nothing left of her. She was in an unreachable world. He remembered how her eyes, misted with release after they made love and lay in bed, had held a hint of lightness, some memory of a trivial amused event. He never asked what she was thinking because he did not want to know.

He wished he had brought along a book to read, like the movie character he had seen in a similar situation. He was trying to recall the name of the movie when she asked him, "What do you want?"

"I want you to remember—"

"Remember what?" She sounded annoyed.

"Your life before you came to this place."

"My life?" Now she turned to face him and he thought he saw a trace of her old energy. "What is it to you?" Her voice was as he recalled it, with a rasp that deepened whenever she was aroused.

He felt ashamed to be thinking of this and he told her once more, "We were friends."

She drew up the cover to her chest and folded her arms. "You are tiring me. I think you should leave."

"It took me two hours to get here," he said gently.

"Then in two hours, you can get back to your home."

He found this funny and for a moment he wondered if this was all an act; an act to punish those she had once known. "Would you like me to return another day?"

"No," she said forcefully, and he recalled their last night together. Will you leave your husband? Are you not unhappy with this situation? Would you like me to walk away? To all his questions, her answer had been the same. No. She stood by her husband and he *did* walk away. At the time he was beginning to feel overwhelmed by her shifting energy. It was also a month or so after he had seen the child on the stairway.

Following his trip to Redrose Manor, he texted the daughter to inform her that the visit had been fruitless and it would not be worthwhile to continue. She replied a day later, thanking him for making the effort; he found this suitably formal.

Yet a month later he was once more on his way to the retirement home. He wondered why he was doing this and he concluded it was the sliver of hidden goodness within him, a lurking decency that was directing his effort. He did not consider that perhaps it was the need to move beyond the another-ness into which she had consigned him. Too much time had passed for that, during which he had been in a longer, more stable relationship; and also, because he truly believed that for men and women of his age, it was remorse rather than pride that was disruptive. Pride was for the young and unformed.

Following his second visit, he did not bother to text the daughter because there was nothing to add. His former lover had reacted in much the same manner as previously, asking him, at the end to leave. A month later it was the same story and more than once he vowed to stop this nonsense, yet in a couple of weeks, he would be again on his way with a bouquet of roses, so red and wanton, so red as to be obscene.

With each visit, he dribbled out more details of their affair and to an onlooker—the caregiver who occasionally hovered at the doorway—the confessions might have seemed somewhat like a sacrament of penance. He mentioned the places where they stole love, drunkenly at times: in a park, in his car, a garden shed, a sofa with coins in its creases. Beneath a trellis wreathed with clematis. Many were public places and at times he felt a twinge of concern, as if so many years later, a concerned neighbour or a cop with a hankering for cold cases would pull up in his driveway and he would have to explain patiently that their affair had broken the surface and they needed to fly higher. He would have to explain that carnality demands ever-expanding risks.

One evening on the train to Redrose Manor, he got an erection. This was not a common occurrence and he would have been pleasantly surprised otherwise, but he felt a deep shame because he was trying to create a narrative with explicit episodes rather than details that might interest a gentle memoirist. He wanted to confront her with the beginning of their affair.

She had been the playful one. Even when she spoke of her husband's coldness, the absence of intimacy, and her suspicions he was wedded to more than his scholarly interests, as she previously believed, her eyes would twinkle with an adolescent's beguilement. She would bring her hands before her, palms on her breasts as she told him of her family, her father as remote as her husband, and her vivacious mother in a relationship with "a gentleman caller." Rupert was his name, and it was only when she was thirteen years old that she understood the nature of their relationship: her mother had been fulfilled by Rupert and her father was freed from further pretenses. Rupert, according to her, was lover of one and friend to the other. One night she told him she could never understand why some women would choose a man so immune to their charms, so remote and diffident, and how some men could live with a woman they have long ceased to understand. A woman flitting like a ghost in an austere house.

At the time he believed he was only a friend, a good listener, and he didn't understand the purpose of her observation. At any rate, he was more curious about her father and her husband. The latter he had observed mostly on his porch chair reading his newspaper or at dinner breaking a loaf with his long, graceful fingers, his handsome face a mystery; the former he imagined dressed in clothes of half a century earlier, doing the same. He wanted to be like both men, handsome, graceful, forgiving, but in the end, he became Rupert.

And in both instances, with him and with Rupert, there had been a child, a witness, the contours of their lives beginning to take shape. Now he recalled the night when he had heard a creak on the stairs and looked up to see outside in the darkness, a child, her hand on the railing. She must have been awakened by her mother's moans, which would have sounded to her like cries of pain. Then the figure was gone. The child's mother under his body had not seen a thing, and he kept quiet because he was not sure if he had imagined the little confused face in the darkness. That month, their last together, he made excuses about his work and begged off visiting.

That was thirty-two years ago. He moved to a house at the other end of the city, and as if to make up for the year and a half of recklessness, he settled into a relationship with a woman who was practical and reserved and prodded him to pay more attention to his career and his health. He lived with her for twelve years until she moved away to another province to take care of her ailing father. His affair seemed a life in parentheses; brief, volatile, and forever canopied by the mundaneness of what came after.

Now he wished he did not have to revisit that period. He decided he would make one last trip to Redrose Manor; he owed that, at least, to the person whose life he had disrupted. On the train, he rehearsed what he would say, but when he entered the room and saw a bouquet of roses on her bedside table, he asked her, "There are fresh roses here. Do you know who brought them?"

Her lips bunched up, wrinkles repeating the heavy lines against her nose. "What concern is that of yours?"

He placed his bouquet flat on the table and saw "to momma" on the card. "It's from your daughter."

For the first time, there was a spark of interest in her wary eyes. "My little girl. I must have been asleep." With her palms, she propped herself higher on the bed. "She walks so quietly, you never know when she's here. Now she's gone." She pointed to him. "What have you done to her?"

"Nothing. I have done nothing." An image of the little face on the stairway burst through his protestation.

Later, he would wonder if people like his former lover—those with scarred memories—were put off by definite statements, preferring uncertainties that mirrored their own confusion. But at that moment, he began to tell her everything. He filled in the details of the places he had previously mentioned. He described her house, the stark paintings on the walls, the lumpen wooden figurine, the beige sofa, the solid piano, the stacked bookcases, and for the first time, saw that her house reflected none of her vivacity.

He went beyond their time together and mentioned his cancer diagnosis and the oncologist's assurance he would die of old age rather than the slow-moving disease. He told her, at last, of her daughter's ghostly figure on the stairway. And finally, he promised her this would be his last visit. She listened patiently and when he was finished, she asked him, "I don't know why you keep coming here. You are only making things worse."

"You know I have been here before, then. Is there anything else you remember?"

"It's not proper for you to be here. What would everyone think?"

Once, her humour had been mischievous and dark, but now when he looked at her face closely, he could see nothing in her eyes, no twist of her lips.

He asked, "Who are you referring to? And why would they think anything?"

"People are always watching and they never forget. Now leave me alone."

He got up. "Do you remember anything of us?"

"You are a foolish man. Why should I remember anything about you? You are just another visitor." Now there was the hint of a smile, but in her drawn and wrinkled face, it appeared almost disdainful.

"I won't return," he told her, his voice lapsing so it seemed a question.

He waited a while for her reply and when there was none, he walked out into the night.

The Magical Cardigan

I live alone in a room I rent from a taciturn man who could be in his late forties or early fifties. He sleeps upstairs but as he's never at home, I know nothing of him other than his affinity for grey sweatshirts, stonewashed jeans, and frayed baseball caps set low over his lean, stubbled face. His attitude is standoffish, and at first I was curious why he decided to rent his room, especially to someone with an accent. I shouldn't complain, because it's spacious and furnished with items abandoned by the previous owner. A creaky bed, a radiogram, a foldup cot, an empty record cabinet, and an oval table pushed against a wall on which there is a triangle of nails. A photograph or mirror would have once hung there.

On the day I moved in, I happened to open the closet and noticed a row of cardigans and matching scarves. The odour of balsamic resin, which sent me back to the Benedictine monastery in Trinidad, suggested that the closet's contents had remained undisturbed for a while. On the lower shelves were an assortment of pink and beige sweaters and a pair of shoes that seemed my size. Most likely the clothes belonged to the couple who were the subjects of the photographs that were arrayed on one wall. Apart from three sepia prints in which they were dressed informally, in the style of the 1940s perhaps, all the pictures were taken late in life, when they were the age I am now.

Some days later, while cleaning the closet I spotted another photograph beneath a half dozen folded sweaters. It was the only representation of the man all by himself. The photograph was taken from a distance, and he looked different. He looked in his early twenties and was in a military uniform, standing on a pier, his hand raised in a salute. I dusted the glass frame and stuck it above the other photos. He appeared too chipper in this pose, gazing down at his older, balder selves holding up a sturgeon, or leaning over a pool table, or reclining on a car, staring at a waterfall. In all of them, his wife stood at his side, his arm around her. I soon realized that what I had mistaken for a salute was really a wave. And it was not jauntiness in his manner either; he was looking at the photographer with a blithe smile, as if this trip were nothing to worry about and he would be back shortly from his military mission. So the woman, though out of the frame, was yet in the scene. Something was different about this one photograph and its subject, though I couldn't say what. During the three months I have been in this place, I have rearranged the photographs several times, according to somewhat arbitrary criteria. I have also organized the cardigans and vests in new combinations, and one night I polished the shoes.

I must find myself a hobby. In the local newspapers, there are notices of seniors' dances and cribbage clubs and casino bus tours. I occasionally try to imagine the neighbourhood couples at these events. In my rendering, the hall is splashed with colourful vests and ringing laughter. Some are waltzing, others exchange snatches of giddy gossip before they move on. In the mornings, they are all more subdued, but they have known each other for ages and can interpret the silence.

I see them on my fortnightly grocery run in the supermarket, or sometimes on the bus. Always well dressed and quietly reflective in the manner of many old people. In the coffee shop opposite the grocery, I observe them through the glass window bringing cups to their lips and cutting their muffins in the daintiest manner. I wonder at their ritual of dressing and whether one fixes the other's collars and sleeves or tucks in an errant shirttail before they leave the house. Do they offer compliments or do they keep their satisfaction to themselves on their way out?

I focus increasingly on someone sitting alone, gazing at some distant object. I want to ask this single person: how do you manage your solitary life? Is the emptiness sometimes redeemed by acceptable memories or do you wish you could have both passed on in adjoining beds? Or maybe I would ask if he—or she—had always been alone, or perhaps on the verge of a marriage before it was called off. But these are not inquiries you make of a stranger.

At night, when I turn off the television after the news, I glance at the couple in the photographs on the wall and I try to imagine their life at the end. A few times, I have placed them in some romantic movie in which the survivor forever carries the memory of the departed. In other instances, I have imagined them growing old and senile together while they wonder at the presence of a stranger in their kitchen. I don't know if it's an obsession, my reflecting on the lives of this departed couple, but after three months, it's easy to believe you share a connection with the faces staring at you every morning. It's the only eye contact I've had in a while. Maybe it's just me growing older, watching the walls close in.

I came to Canada eight years ago, although it seems much longer. A beneficiary of the government's desperation over the imminent elections, I took the early retirement package offered to anyone over fifty-five, one of the many bribes thrown to the public, and I decided to travel. The party eventually lost the elections, but I was in Canada by then, in the fixer-upper with my niece, my brother's only child, and her husband and son. The boy was three at the time and even though I was not comfortable staying with the family, they persuaded me to extend my visit. They spoke about renovating the house and the cost of labour and made jokes I could not understand about taxi drivers and the city's mayor and other politicians.

The jokes were short-lived, and they never renovated, but driven both by the memory of my dead brother and by the reduced rent, I stayed with them for five years, fixing the plumbing, repairing the basement, restoring furniture bought at garage sales, and babysitting. That must have been their plan all along and looking back, I am annoyed by my acquiescence, especially as this situation was awkward for someone who had lived alone for most of his life. But the years passed, and I was neither surprised nor distressed when they went their separate ways, although I never expected, as part of the arrangement, to wait with the boy at Union Station for one or the other parent to collect him. For whatever spiteful reason, they did not want to meet, and I guess that was better than having a big public argument.

When I turned sixty-five three months ago, I resigned from the factory and moved to Oshawa. There was a moment of panic when my niece inquired whether I would still act as a minder of the boy as before, and I explained the length of journey several times before she understood that it was impossible.

I grew up in an average-sized family. There were six of us, including my parents. By the time I turned thirteen, there were four of us, and at twenty-two, the year I moved out, just three. When my brother migrated to Canada following the death of our mother, I returned to the family house. I was there when I heard the news of his death. I was an accountant at the Ministry of Transportation at the time and I did not presume the passing of my entire family made me special—there were several survivors like me in the neighbourhood, men and women in their mid-forties whose relatives had been carried away by diabetes or heart failure or bullets. None, though, was living alone in a house with so many empty rooms.

There is a phrase that beats around my head. Fate stepped in between me and my life. Or my lie, or love, and I cannot recall where I first heard it said. I may have made it up, I had enough cause, but that was a lifetime away. If, in my youth, someone had told me that at sixty-five, I would live in a single room, alone and friendless in another country, I would have laughed.

But if my prescience was faulty, I can look back with crystal clarity. I no longer try to form connections between what I missed and what might lie before me. There are no connecting threads; life is what it is and there is no reason to expect anything other than what we are daily presented. All the little rituals, the habits that become a second skin, serve a single unspectacular purpose: to take us neatly to the end.

Yet we resist. We resist even when we understand the folly of doing so.

Ten days ago, I tried out the clothes from the closet. The cardigans smelt of mothballs and the vests were stretched out in the middle but they fitted me reasonably well. The first three days, I wore them only inside the room, occasionally glancing at myself in the mirror. One midmorning, I fell asleep in one of these striped vests. When I awoke, I imagined the couple's eyes on me and I scanned the photographs to locate the vest. It was not there, but I was shaken, nonetheless.

The next day I took a cardigan for a test run around the block. At the coffee shop, I noticed a woman gazing at me through the glass window, and in the grocery, a middle-aged man glanced up from his shopping cart as I passed. It was a fleeting look, but I wondered whether this old dark grey cardigan with loose knitting at the cuffs carried the old owner's spirit. Some remnants of his temperament. But by the time I made the block, I decided that likely, they assumed I'd bought the worn item from the Salvation Army.

The next day I chose another cardigan, this one in better condition, burgundy with leather elbow patches designed, I presume, to go along with a plaid hat and a pipe. This outfit was more distinctive than the previous day's and I decided that curious glances from strangers rather than from people in my neighbourhood might be more tolerable, so I headed to the Oshawa GO station. From habit, I got off at Union. From habit, too, I surveyed the lines before the pastry shops and the fast-food joints and settled on a bench offering a view of the schedules board overhead. There had been renovations since my last visit and everyone appeared to be in a hurry: the youthful men with their blue jerseys striding to the Air Canada Centre, young women in tights and varsity jackets dragging their suitcases to the Via Rail stairs, couples rushing to the adjoining subway station.

Because the place was so crowded, these people rushing here and there sometimes brushed each other's arms. I closed my eyes, and I wondered what these fleeting contacts would give to a person wearing a magical cardigan. A whiff of a memory long forgotten? I must have smiled at the thought, and I heard a nearby giggle. When I opened my eyes, the owner of the giggle, a teenager in a beanie tuque, asked me, "Have you seen Mr Rogers? From the old TV show?"

I was about to answer when I spotted the mischievous grin on her companion, another teenager with rabbit ears and red fuzzy growth on his pointed chin. I closed my eyes once more and did not flinch when Mr Rabbitears whispered something about an "old man hipster." I have to say that I find young people unnecessarily frivolous. I reflected on this during my return journey. The train was packed with teenage girls. It may have been the cowboy hats and torn jeans they were wearing, but they all appeared to resemble each other. They were shouting and singing and I concluded from their excited conversations that they were returning from a concert featuring a country singer whose outfit they must have been imitating. Not for the first time, I felt like an interloper. Perhaps if I had a child or children of my own, my mood would have been different.

When I got off the train at Oshawa, it was drizzling a little. It was the beginning of May, and the droplets seemed to melt as they touched my skin. The effect was of walking in a more humid climate, and I recalled my life in a distant country, at a distant time. The humidity there was like a tightening coat on particularly sweltering days, but in the cool misty mornings it loosened a shimmering magic that disguised colours and softened aluminium roofs. During that brief period, an hour at the most, it was not impossible to imagine music, a faint tinny sound, from the wreathed trees and passing cars and the ever-present vines that seemed to fluff and reform with the mist.

Five years ago, when I was staying with my niece and her family, a man in his late sixties, wearing a grey bespoke suit, was saying on TV that the mind forever tries to bury offending events. But nothing can be buried forever, he'd recited, shaking his perfectly coiffured head. On another station, another man, younger and bulkier in his loose, thuggish T-shirt, had pronounced that we are made and unmade by a single decision, though we never see it at the time.

These recollections puzzled me. As I walked on, I wondered whether they were associated with the sudden end of the only substantial relationship in my life. But that was half a lifetime away, and I had for a long time put aside my fiancée's decision to call off our engagement. She had been increasingly worried by the mortality rate in my family and did not want to be a widow in her thirties. There is a particular island scene: we were returning from a trip to the Mount St Benedict's chapel and the rain lathering the windscreen gave an air of unreality to what she was saying. I want a better guarantee, she had said when she stepped out of the car into the storm. With the wind whipping her hair, she enumerated the qualities she wanted in a husband. I possessed none—money, good genes, stability—but I had seen nervousness in her eyes, not callousness. Her list was not meant to cut, but to emphasize that it was truly over. In retrospect, I cannot fault her logic. She was married soon after to the son of a wealthy businessman. But I had survived. Thirty-four years have passed since she left my car door open in her hurry to get to her house, the wind slamming it shut before I could reach over to say I understood her decision.

I assumed the drizzle had stopped, but as I passed a streetlamp, I observed the drops, discoloured by the light, resembling a clutch of tiny insects flung against the breeze. The wind picked up, and I buttoned my cardigan and turned up the collar. I tested the inner lining, lambskin most likely, soft and warm against my body. As I watched the cars streaming by, their headlights capturing the pattern of raindrops, I wondered if the cardigan's actual owner was ever inflicted with this kind of melancholia.

It's surprising how an idle thought, childish and irrational, can take hold of us sometimes. When I was a child, I had listened to stories of spirits passing their yearnings onto the bodies of hosts who had uncovered a private artifact, like a diary. But they were not only children's stories, because following each death, priests had been summoned to bless our house to cure it of its voraciousness. During these rituals, when water was sprinkled and mysterious words mumbled, I hoped the spirits would not be assuaged; that some imprint of my dead relatives might survive the exorcism.

When I walked out of the rain into the familiarity of my room, I imagined it was the weather—the rain and the washed-out colours and the little ruffle of humidity—that had provoked these memories. I dried my hair and sat on a chair before the oval table and the triangle of nails. I tried to imagine my room under different circumstances. There would be a photograph of my parents, my father unsmiling, my mother with her eyes cast down. And just beneath, my siblings. They would be young in the photos because they had passed away so early. Maybe, too, there might be a photograph of me with curly-hair grandchildren scattered around.

An hour later, I got up and poked around the closet as if I would, once more, find a lost photograph, this one of a young woman clutching the hem of her summer dress and gazing at the city with such intensity that a passerby might have imagined this could be the last time she would see it. Or another photograph, taken less than an hour later, the woman hurrying out of a car, the man's hand outstretched as if trapped in uncertain midgesture. I fell asleep with the images circling each other.

Something is different this morning. I cannot say what it is, apart from the fact that I awoke later than usual. On the street, I try to recall the dream of the previous night. I had fallen asleep with the same cardigan with which I am now outfitted. It either fits me better than the others or I am just getting used to its texture and shape. I do not get off the train at Union, and as it speeds along all the towns—Mimico, Long Branch, Port Credit, Appleby, Aldershot—I experience a new curiosity about the inhabitants hidden beyond the rushing scrubs. Is it possible that in a small joint somewhere, sitting alone, is a man of my age, his life marked by similar disappearances? I try to picture this man.

The following days, I extend my trips, shifting from train to bus. And with each trip, I add a detail to the man of my age, sitting alone. He is slim, smallish, and forever considering distance over his clasped hands. And he is wearing a cardigan that matches mine. He is a man of several races and rejected by each, he feels no affiliation to any.

One afternoon, I drop off at Hamilton. There is an old-style diner inside the station and I order a coffee and a double bacon sandwich. The following day I find myself in Guelph, where I have a poutine meal. The food swirls heavily in my stomach during my return trip, and by the time I get to the apartment, I am in a hurry to use the washroom. The landlord is sitting on the porch smoking, and it's awkward to rush past him with a hurried hello. When I glance out fifteen minutes later, he is gone.

The following week, I continue my journey, choosing places that previously had held no interest. A bookstore in Picton, a lighthouse in Port Hope, a Maple Festival in Elmira, an art gallery in Grimsby. I walk along streets with limestone houses and cottages that seem plucked from another time. Away from the cities, I observe settlements nestled between forests, and ridges separating farmlands. I purchase trivial items from farmers' markets stocked with jars of honey and home-baked bread and cuts of meat and trays of fruits and vegetables. In the nights, I go over all the places I visited and try to recall particular sights, the gardens and heritage homes or the angles of hilly streets or the way a tree brushes the face of a church. I attempt to envision the men who built these places, their attire, the meals they ate, their conversations, the thoughts swirling through their minds when they gazed at the finished structures. I imagine, too, the communities forever displaced by the imposition of progress. Change is never even.

Maybe it's the remoteness, but I do not feel like an intruder or an outsider in any of these places, nor am I bothered when I consider someone noticing my conversation with an invisible companion. I believe each day I am learning something new about the actual owner of the cardigan and it occurs to me that I could be writing his obituary, adding a line with each trip. It's a curious notion.

I now look forward to these excursions, which is strange because they are so different from the solitary life into which I had squeezed myself. There is so much from which I had skittered away, ignoring the mysteries right around the corner. I reflect on this during my stops and I think the disaffection of the last few years was a way of dealing with all the premature departures in my life. That may or may not be true, but I find myself looking at the women as I had not done for a decade, sly appraising glances they never catch but which are long enough for me to get a sense of their moods. I imagine walking across and introducing myself. "Hi. I couldn't help noticing the cover of the book you are reading. It reminds me of . . . " It's a new, exhilarating experience. One afternoon, while I am returning from Parry Sound and gazing through the train window at the jagged Georgian Bay coastline and marvelling at the rugged picturesqueness, I wonder if the owner of the cardigan I am wearing travelled these routes and if, like me, his eyes had opened to a world he had previously annulled.

In the island from which I had arrived, because of the varying shades of green and brown, everything arrayed before us blended: the houses into the roads, the roads into the ravines, the ravines into the forests, the forests into the sky, the sky into the ocean. But in the scene before me now, everything seems to have been ripped from another place and hurled with frightful force. It brings to mind those religious myths of warring gods and thunderbolts and fierce unending fires. The effect is a terrible blemished beauty, a mangled grandeur I cannot fit into words. (Or rather, one I cannot comprehend and so can only represent awkwardly. I think of arterial ruptures and fissures, and crags that resemble teeth.)

From my recent habit, I try to see the landscapes through the eyes of the owner of the cardigan. But he had his wife; and his view would not have been his alone. They would have pointed out landmarks and sitting side by side each would have borrowed from the other's mood. I try again but it does not work, and I realize this vision for which I am reaching, in spite of my pretenses, would always be fraudulent; always beyond my reach.

Loneliness in a place of stark beauty is an awful thing; the setting inflames an indefinable sorrow that hovers around like a taint or a sacrilege. There is an incandescent feeling of loss and emptiness. Perhaps we have evolved to share—or, by sharing. A kind of reciprocal altruism. I sense my mood of the last weeks shifting; and by the time the bus stops at Barrie, I feel like an interloper, or worse, a hypocrite. There is a great sorrow that this landscape has stripped away the expansive freedom I'd conjured while visiting the small towns, eating in their diners, walking on their streets, gazing at their monuments and museums. All gone. Gone.

I imagine the cardigan shrinking and the threads cutting into my flesh. I suffer on the train and I cannot wait to get to the apartment. Once there, I tear it off and fling it on the bed. Following my prolonged bath, I stare at the bed and I say to the cardigan, "What have you wrought?" The silliness of the words eases my malaise and I laugh uneasily. "The magic is gone," I add, as if there were a giggling audience beneath the bed or hiding in the closet. It's a foolish thought, but unexpectedly, it frightens me. I examine the closet, and with some difficulty, I check under the bed.

I find sections of rolled carpet, and what appears to be a metal scooper, and a toolbox. I cannot crawl beneath the bed, so I get a rack from the closet and I pull the toolbox toward me. When I open it, I see a batch of airmail envelopes bound with elastic bands. They are diaphanous and bleached blue and the handwriting—elegantly slanted and carefully punctuated—is the same on each airmail. It seems a woman's hand but I am not sure. For the last three months, I had gazed at the photographs on the walls and I had tried to imagine the lives of the couple; I had spent close to three weeks wandering around the place pretending I could somehow imbibe some sensibility of the man in the photograph, but now, presented with an opportunity to learn about the couple, I do not know what I should do. I get up and sit on the bed and I think if this were a movie or a novel, I would uncover some secret, a special insight to rub away my unexpected unease from earlier in the day. But I also worry that it's private and never meant for another person's eyes, certainly not mine. Not an interloper's.

Early the next morning I glance at the envelopes and remove the bands.

The following day, I see the owner of the house on the porch. I am returning from the grocery and I am tired from the walk and the weight of the bags. He flicks away his cigarette, rushes down the steps and helps me with a bag. He says there is a community bus that comes every hour at a nearby intersection, and I realize he believes me to be much older than I am. But I *am* old and I am panting. I place the other bag on the ground. He talks about his job as a landscaper and losing his license three years earlier. He had been speeding and there had been an injury. He lights another cigarette and pulls his cap lower. I wait for him to elaborate. From his hesitation and the way he is shifting his feet and altering his stance, I assume he is considering a confession. Instead, he says, "You no longer wear dad's cardigan."

Surprised, I stutter out a reply. "It's too hot now. I hope you didn't mind."

"Oh no. I am glad it's some use." He takes a deep drag from his cigarette. "Been meaning to clean out the place for a while . . . I may have to sell soon. I can't afford the mortgage."

"Didn't your parents own the house?"

"They did, but we were forced to re-mortgage when dad had

his heart attack. I was rushing mom to the hospital when I had the accident."

"I am sorry," I say and feel a hypocrite to be thinking of my circumstance during the recounting of his tragedy.

"It's been a while." He flicks the cigarette in a neat arc. His gaze gets distant, and he adds, "Mom always said she didn't want to outlast two husbands. Her first husband . . . or it may have been her fiancée, as her story was never straight . . . he died in the war." He turns from the wind, cups his palm but does not light the cigarette he has withdrawn from the pack on the rail. "She got her wish." After a while, I take my bags from the ground and walk into the house. Did he not know? And if not, should I be the one to tell him? I circle the room, looking at the photos on the wall as if a face might nod or frown. On my bed, I continue staring at the faces, my eyes drawn to the waving soldier at the pier.

Half an hour later, I return to the porch with the toolbox. "I found these beneath the bed. I was cleaning up. I don't know who they are from." I feel guilty about the lie. He takes the toolbox from me and places it on the railing. "Yeah. Don't know if I want to read them. Mom never spoke much about her first husband." But he flicks through the lot. "It's from her. Hmm, look at the date here. And there aren't any stamps. Now, why would she do that?" He seems confused.

"There's a newspaper clipping," I tell him. I do not reveal it's an obituary.

I wait for a while. "It makes no sense." He has the obituary in one hand and a letter in the other. I say nothing. He will figure it out himself.

It's close to the end of the month now. I have already packed my things in cardboard boxes, ready for my next move. I hope it will be my last. I have replaced all but one cardigan in the manner I found them and I have cleaned out the room. I gaze at the photograph of the soldier I fixed against the triangle of nails where it must have once hung. I have not seen his son for a week and I don't know whether he has changed his plans about selling. Still, I walk around the neighbourhood, looking at places that might house an old man with no connections. During one of these trips, I feel a tap on my shoulder. I turn, a bit startled.

"I recognized the sweater." He grins through his stubbles. "What are you doing in this neighbourhood? It's a little rough."

"It's only half an hour from your place."

"Yeah." We walk together and he says, "I have lived here for most of my life. Who would have guessed there were secrets right beneath my feet?"

I guess he is thinking of the line in the obituary: *"Corporal S— died heroically in battle. He leaves behind his pregnant and grieving wife."* "Life is like that," I tell him.

"Yeah. My . . . my father said that sometimes. You never know."

"You never know what?"

He looks at me and, for the briefest of moments, there is a spark of interest in his eyes. Then he pulls his cap low over his forehead and says, "I'm heading to the pub."

"My drinking days are over."

He grins and we part ways. As I approach the house, I feel I should have joined him. Maybe the liquor would have loosened my throat and I would have revealed that I had been searching far and wide for a local version of myself, a solitary man emptied by regrets but right here in the room, there had been someone—not a man but a woman—who had been living two lives. One like the crowd in the groceries and coffee shops. And the other like mine.

The Teak Toy Trunk

I used to be unexpectedly moved by the dutiful condolences of strangers. Young couples mostly who recognized me from news reports and who, for a minute or two, offered hurried tidbits from their own brief lives as a preamble to their awkward, commingled pity. A few offered hugs but tentatively, as if closeness might taint them, too, with bad luck. In time, I learned to turn away. I have read that grief makes us more empathetic, but I believe it also freezes a part of our soul.

In those early days, I allowed my features to reflect those of the gazers—so lost I was! My therapist at the time, one of the few holdovers from the flurry of court-appointed officials, said I should resist this mirroring—the term that rolled off her tongue was *echopraxia*—because it demonstrated a deeper journey towards self-denial. She was a petite woman, always smartly dressed in striped suits, and accentuating her recommendations with crisp birdlike gestures that gave an element of theatre to the sessions. But she was efficient and, towards the end, ruthless. These sessions were unfruitful not only because I had, at an earlier time, made myself averse to anything that sounded like prescriptive badgering, but because I was not ready to streamline my life. I think I drew comfort from the medley of voices, accusing, comforting, and sometimes speaking with intonations that could indicate either. I suppose I was afraid of clarity, which I saw during one session as a straight line of knives. In any event, I was not prepared to move on. I really was not.

That was four years ago, and in the early mornings before the sun rose, I would stand by the window and gaze for hours at the city into which I had escaped two decades earlier and which offered everything I had hoped for me and my daughter. I would observe the sunlight bouncing from one glass building to the next, shattering and reforming the landscape, stealing its familiarity. And looking down from my window, I struggled each day to understand this place that gave life to my child and then pulled it away. Soon, my view altered, and I saw only emptiness. A frozen wasteland. I fought this hollowness, tried to fill it with inspirational books, and I discovered how easily unstable sorrow could shift into an expanding void that sucked away every ounce of energy. Emptiness feeding on emptiness: it was like being trapped in a permanent limbo. Once I had asked my therapist why the absence of something, grief, in this case, could spread into a slow deflation of everything else and she allowed her fingers to flutter over her pad and, almost imperceptibly, rolled her eyes. What do you remember the most of your daughter? she had asked, eventually.

There is a particular insolence that is a wonderful thing to observe from a distance; to see how its complementary fragments—boldness, defiance, recklessness, fragility—meld into eyes wary of the world and lips set against intrusiveness. Though I never saw it myself, the residents of the townhouse apartment we shared, my daughter and I, had commented on our resemblance. I suppose they were referring to our mannerisms because of her aquiline features and slightly slouching frame she inherited from her father. In the immediate aftermath of our child's death, before the hollowness set in, I prayed for familiarity, for connection, however tenuous. But with her father, there had been neither.

L— will be visiting from his island home one week from now and it will be the first time I will see him in twenty-four years. If his email had arrived a year earlier, I would have stated bluntly that I preferred he maintain his distance; it is easy to imagine that he would not have been too surprised, because that was how he knew me in the months before my hasty and unplanned escape from the island. Twenty-four years ago, the airmail letters took two weeks to arrive and his first letters were suffused with self-pity that unexpectedly broke off into scattershot threats but thankfully, once he determined I would never return, the threats were replaced with bland evocations of karma. "God's will," was a phrase constantly repeated, as was the sentence, "I leave everything in God's hands." There was never any mention of our daughter because he did not know then, nor does he know now, of his fleeting role in her existence.

There have been three recent emails from him, the first a gentle inquiry whether I was the Z— who had moved from the island two decades earlier; the second, slightly longer, a compendium of hurriedly snatched quotes about loss and grief; and the third, an itinerary of his trip to Toronto. It was only to his last email that I replied. I thanked him for his compilation of quotes and wished him an enjoyable trip. Following this email, I dug out the airmail letters he had written in the past, at a different time in our lives. I had bundled them together with double rubber bands and tucked them away at the bottom of a teak toy trunk. I was mildly surprised at the air both of permanence and of fragility conveyed by the pale blue diaphanous paper on which they were written. It was only when I was sorting them that I realized L— had misstated when I had left the island; of my entire collection of letters, his were the only ones from someone I knew.

I replaced the sgraffito and the other murals my daughter had done as school assignments, together with more recently purchased books and folders atop the trunk, which I pushed once more to the side of the sofa. I bundled his letters with the others I had received from strangers. Some I had read so often that particular phrases had stuck in my mind and others, read only once, were so accusatory I would never forget their bite. During the period when I had begun to ritualize and streamline my life, I separated the supportive letters into two categories: the ones that commiserated the loss of a daughter in an almost academic manner, and those that were faltering and earnest but which always ended with a confession from the writers saying they would never truly know if such a void could be filled.

Soon after she died, my mind had been filled with fantasies of revenge on the thugs who could not care whether their spray of bullets directed at a rival, who escaped unharmed, might cut down an innocent bystander venturing out of the club for a cigarette. And when these revenge fantasies had run their course and left me with nothing but certain knowledge of my helplessness, my thoughts turned to suicide. It seemed such a straightforward way to end my misery that for weeks I carried around a cocktail of medication that was not unduly difficult for someone in my position to procure. It was only the fear that the three young men, grinning as they were led away by the police, might be released if I, too, were gone that gave a dull purpose to my days.

And I filled those days with meaningless activities that exhausted me to such a degree that in the nights I fell asleep on the couch or at the kitchen table with a duster or cleaning pad in my hand. I swept, scoured and sanitized every inch of the apartment. I repainted, dragged furniture out of their corners, started a garden, and tilled the soil so often the earthworms came up in bits. One night while I was carrying groceries across the street, I was almost hit by a bus; afterwards, when unpacking my purchases on the kitchen table, I laughed, for the first time since my daughter's death, at the cruel headlines that might occur to an inventive editor. Perhaps: *Mother follows Daughter*, or, *Unlucky Family or Cursed*?

I never mentioned this to the therapist because I had begged off all our recent sessions, but I was determined the headline would never be written. So the next morning, I wrote out a routine I stuck on the fridge. Such a simple thing, but it was this routine that preserved me. Soon my days became more streamlined, my mind trained—or tricked—into a rigidity of purpose that allowed little or no space for the turbulence of unnecessary activities or emotions. And through this sequencing, I finally found the strength to step out. I granted belated interviews to journalists I had turned away previously. I contacted parents paralysed by tragedies. The time I had spent cleaning I now used to write letters to newspapers and groups. I was invited to speak to some of these organizations and I was occasionally photographed carefully attired, smiling, composed, a glass of wine sometimes in my hand. I became a public figure, my address out there.

And so, the second category of letters. Even though close to two years had passed since the death, I was someone who did not fit the image of a grieving woman. I was not pious, my face not streaked with ashes, and worse, I was using this tragedy to bask in the limelight. These letters, bilious, occasionally bigoted, seemed to have tapped a nerve that sprung from a different century; another location. Most were from men, but a few were signed by women and the rancour in these suggested that I had brought dishonour to every mother and daughter.

At first, I pushed those aside into their separate stack, intending to reply to them but decided against this because I lost interest in defending myself to those who, knotted by their invisible burdens, would never listen to anything I had to say. If this sounds mean-spirited, my only defence is that I was intent on preserving my sanity.

At the side of the teak toy trunk is my little bookshelf filled with books, fiction mostly and written by women from other continents. At one time, I unexpectedly found comfort in a travelogue written by a feisty woman who, a century ago, journeyed to Arabia and to Afghanistan. I pretended that each step she took not only set her on the brink of a new world but also erased a bit of her past. This night I hold it on my lap, unopened, waiting for the assurances I once received from this traveller who set her own path. But the memories loosened from the contents of the trunk—the memorabilia and the letters—get in the way.

But perhaps it's the trunk itself.

I had first spotted it at a garage sale, rows of dolls set upon its solid frame. My daughter was in the car with me and it was she, four at the time, who pointed it out at the end of the lawn, close to the street. While I was paying for the dolls, my attention was drawn to the trunk which, with its brass handle and side straps, looked like a pirate's chest. The owner must have noticed my attention because she opened the lid to display an engraved image of a phoenix. I got it at a steal because the hinges were rusted and the varnish had long since peeled away. I planned on using it as an archive for my treasured books, but my daughter immediately claimed it. In time, it was filled with whatever interested her at the moment, and following her death I saw, scattered at the top, term papers and notes for her constantly shifting dissertation.

When the trunk was empty, she used to hide there to surprise me, and even now, I feel a whiff of her presence, an odour, an imagined texture, a shattered symphony straining within. (If I sound too florid, it's only because I sometimes feel that within is a record of my daughter's life and death, shrunk to fit the trunk's dimension.)

It strikes me that L— would understand what the condemning letter-writers would not. He would see the photographs and recognize a woman who had begun, years ago, to reform herself on an island where minor liberties were always seen as transgressive. He would see the poise not as coldness, or worse, as calculative, but as a way of hardening oneself in a society where backbiting, like one of the regular storms, tore everything in its path. He would recall our conversations of the months before my departure, the flurry of accusations and counter-accusations that somehow always ended with me being compared with his family members, aunts and mothers, all chaste and obedient. So and so would never do this, or so and so had advised him to be careful of a woman who argued like a man. Once I told him that the people who are the most oppressed often put up the most eloquent defences because they needed some stock reason to justify their weakness, and the face of which he was so proud grew rubbery and weak. Yet I remained with him; it was only when one night he had crept into our apartment, drunk and garrulous, boasting that he was like everyone else, all his friends and cousins in his drinking and liming and his weekend fishing trips that I finally thought of escape. He was right in his invocation of a culture where absolute carefreeness, *dokaydamn*, a counterweight to the rigidity of the old plantations, was admired. This realization made things worse rather than reassuring for me. But where could I go?

A month and a half later, following a visit to my gynecologist, her office decorated with degrees from York University and McMaster in Ontario, I withheld one decision and leaped to another. I told him nothing of the visit to the doctor but mentioned that I was thinking of visiting an aunt in Toronto. (In reality, there was no aunt, but he knew so little of me.)

And so the quarrels conducted late in the nights when his drunkenness gave him an unstable but interminable energy. The island, he said, was passing through an oil boom, his wealthy family expected marriage and children, people would "say things." He had planned to get me a car, and so on. And every argument he put up hardened my mind against him and his island. "What happen to you?" he asked one night. "What change you so?" It was the one time I almost told him of my visit to the doctor. But I did not; at the time I was not thinking of connections but the opposite.

If I now agree to meet L—, he will likely be even more perturbed by what the last few years have wrought, but twenty-four years after his questions, I convince myself I have nothing to add.

The week goes by quickly, and with each passing day, his three emails seem like a version of one of the drunken stunts—threats—he used to pull. One day, I return to my apartment to see the answering machine blinking. I slip off my boots, remove a leaf snagged by a heel, and fill the kettle. While the water is boiling, I listen to the messages, the first two from telemarketers, each hello more accented than the last, and the final message punctuated with long pauses and a stammering request.

I make my tea and sit at the kitchen table. I have absent-mindedly placed the leaf into the bowl of nectarines and kiwis. The leaves of the larch and dogwood and hedge maple outside my kitchen window are falling with each tuft of breeze, and soon I will have to rake and gather them in bags. The willow, meanwhile, carries on like a grumpy old aunt. Once I believed fall was the most morose of seasons, but now I am thankful for the change of *any* season. It may sound silly but I believe that in the tropics, grief, just like the vines that shroud so many trees, thickens from the humidity, takes root with the rain, and lengthens with the unending sun. But here, four times every year, I am made aware of burgeoning changes. Nothing is left uninterrupted. Even sorrow.

I replay the last message. He is staying at a Comfort Inn and would like to meet before he leaves for Montreal. "I have a few things I want to do," is the last sentence, and I am reminded of the island's abruptness. The next evening, there is a new message. Each day, there is another. They are all variations of the first and I wonder what it is he has to do. An old habit of conjecturing returns and I am irritated by L—'s closeness. I decide to let him proceed to Montreal; I have nothing to say to him.

One evening, there is a longer message. It is accentuated with pauses and sniffles, but I can determine that he will depart by train the next day and he would like to meet at the rail station. The train leaves at six PM and he must check out of his room at eleven AM. I leave my work early. At a food court downtown, I have a coffee. The place is brightly lit and most of the women are outfitted in sweaters and scarves. A sea of blues and greys, although the younger women are wearing chiffon blouses, a bit of vividness before winter takes over. The men sitting opposite, their jackets strung on the chairs, are nodding, smiling occasionally, folding and refolding their arms. Every single time I have been presented with these quiet scenes, I think these people are either at peace or skillful at hiding their anxieties.

I glance at my watch, the time moving from twelve to half-past to one. I still have not decided if I would go. But at two-thirty, I get up and walk up the stairs toward Union Station. The place is crowded and a few women glance at me, though I feel it's because of the blankness in my face; and suddenly my belt feels too tight, the strap on my purse too long, my shoes a size smaller. At the terminal, unlike at the food court, there aren't any couples, just solitary travellers. It is the weekend before Thanksgiving and they seem distressed, as if they have been reluctantly pushed into these trips. Journeys nowadays, I think, though conducted through more efficient means, are not the things of pleasure and expectations they used to be. A few students are slouching on the bench to fiddle with their phones and laptops. As I glance around, I am held by the hope that L— has somehow changed his mind, but I see him at the far end, holding a newspaper close to his face. He is wearing a hat and a London Fog trench coat and as I walk towards him, I notice his extra weight and the grey stubble on his face. I say hello and sit two seats away. He takes his time to fold his newspaper and when he lifts his head to stare before him, I see that the additional pounds have altered the contours of his face, so he appears a man in repose. I was expecting something else, though what exactly I cannot say.

He tells me I have not changed, although he has barely looked at me. There is an uncertainty in his voice, a whittling away of his words that do not match his pose. He folds his newspaper on his lap and says nothing for a while. I try to find words and I tell him I hope he is enjoying his trip. He nods but a trifle impatiently and I realize he has something to declare. He tells me he won't be staying too long in Montreal because he has to get back to the island. He unrolls the newspaper and I glimpse his handwriting on a crossword puzzle before he pushes it into the flap of his travelling bag. There are no suitcases at his feet. You are travelling light, I say to him.

Once more he nods and as he pulls his coat around him, I try to see the talkative, confident and selfish person I knew. An oldish man on the opposite bench opens his eyes and I feel he would not know what to make of us. Nor do I. Why do you want this meeting? I ask. He seems relieved by the question. He talks a bit about the island. Millionaires are popping up all over the place, but they live in barricaded palaces because of the kidnappings. It's impossible to say who the real criminals are, he adds. Where to lodge your sympathy.

This is a new way of talking for him and I say I have lost touch because I don't follow the news. It's not all bad, he replies. In the villages, life goes on the way it always did. He describes a festival he had attended some time ago and the street food he had bought and I relax. We are nothing more than two people meeting briefly to chat about a place with which we share a connection. The man opposite opens his eyes once more and wipes the corner of his lips. I notice his zipper is halfway down and I hope his visit is to his children or a grandchild. And during this moment of distraction, L— asks if I ever wondered if things might have turned out differently if I had not left the island.

I am about to ask what precisely he is referring to, but I know what he means. I know because it's a question I've often posed myself. So there is no hesitation in my response. Death has a hundred hands and walks by a thousand ways. He seems confused, so I explain that it's a line by a poet that I came upon during my period of grief. I will never know and it's pointless to speculate. I prefer instead to think of the person *my* daughter—I almost slip here—had been during her twenty years. I prefer to savour the memories and be thankful she was, however briefly, a part of my life. When I realize I am repeating phrases used by my therapist, I stop.

You were always strong, he says. I am surprised and want to look at his face. He nudges his travelling bag closer with his foot and glances at the flashing dial on the wall. I will just be a day in Montreal. An old friend.

I am irritated by my curiosity about this old friend. As I prepare to leave, I wish him once more a happy trip. Or the rest of it. I wonder what he had been doing in his hotel all week.

Perhaps he knows what I am thinking and says he could not get a flight to correspond with his Montreal visit, so he had to spend a few days in Toronto. I am not sure I believe him and I wonder why he would make the effort to lie. It's complicated, he says after a while.

His voice is different but the evasiveness is familiar and suddenly I wish to leave.

He glances at a young woman, in her early twenties, coming up the stairs, a phone clapped to her ear. As she passes us, I notice her winsome smile as if she were imagining a reunion and rearranging herself to match the child she once was. She goes along, talking loudly and happily. Now, for the first time, he leans forward and turns to me and I am shocked at how exhausted he appears. There are yellow flecks in his eyes and his face—contented in profile—now seems rubbery. His lips have been pushed inward by his fleshy cheeks and his jaw has receded a bit. I will be gone soon, he says. There is a tear trickling down an eye. It seems unnatural and I wait for the other eye to catch up. And while I wait, I find myself dropping words of comfort. Small words, the kind that used to annoy me at one time. Yet he seems disappointed when I stop. It's as if he had been waiting here all this time, at the train station, and in his Comfort Inn for me to say this.

He tells me he had been collecting all the articles about my daughter's death, but when an announcement drowns out his words, he seems relieved. And so am I, immeasurably. Following the announcement, there is a rush of people from one entrance and the departure of those sitting on the benches. A woman in her thirties walks towards the senior sitting opposite us. She takes the older man's suitcase.

I get up with him and walk to the ticket counter. He offers his hand and says if I feel like visiting the island within the next month or two, I should let him know. There are three couples ahead and the ticket agent is explaining something to a man who seems not to understand. I feel awkward to be standing with him in silence, but feel it would be rude to walk away, and for a minute,

I consider telling him about his daughter. We have revealed nothing of each other and once again, I wonder at the real purpose of his visit. A young man comes up to the senior at the counter and whispers to the agent.

He tells me that the young man is the son and although I cannot see the resemblance between the two men, one slim and tall and the other short and compact, he says that they share the same features. It's not difficult to see, he adds. With practice, you develop this skill.

The agent beckons with his finger, and L— reaches into his travelling bag and produces an envelope next to the newspaper. He holds it before me and because he is about to go and because the agent seems annoyed, I take it. If it had been offered while we were on the bench, I would have deferred. He walks through the exit without glancing back. I make my way through the station and I find myself suddenly annoyed by all the renovations, the mazes and corridors. When I get home, I am exhausted and I place the envelope in the teak trunk. I sit for a while to catch myself.

Three months later, I see a notice in a community newspaper. I am about to turn the page when I glimpse a name. I take it to my desk. It's not the practice for deaths in other places to be included in the local newspapers unless they are of important people and it takes a while before I determine the true reason for its placement. I retrieve the envelope I had placed in the teak trunk and I see newspaper clippings of our daughter, each accompanied by photographs. I walk to the garden with the newspaper. The damp cold seeps through my coat, and I feel it beneath my skin. It's the worst kind of cold, but if I stay out long enough, my body will gradually adjust. A forlorn gull is flying overhead. Something seems wrong with its wing, but it stabilizes as it soars, riding an air current, and when I can no longer see it, I return to the house.

I cut out the obituary, and before I place it in the envelope, I glance at the lines that had caught my attention. . . . *died from pancreatic cancer . . . He was predeceased by his daughter . . . Together, they are in a better place . . .*

Decades

He had always measured his life in decades. When he was ten, he was sent to live with elderly relatives in a town close to his high school. At twenty, he began to drink heavily with an assortment of petty criminals. Thirty, in another country, married with a young son and another child on the way. Forty, divorced and aspiring to recreate his bachelor lifestyle. In the following decade, he watched the children grow into strangers while still hoping the transition from muralist to landscape painter would pay off. And at sixty, the start of his health problems that were not due to the cancer on his mother's side or the diabetes on his father's but a neurological issue he knew nothing about.

An arteriovenous malformation it was called or an AVM—the abbreviation reminding him of a movie studio with strolling, robed extras—and it was diagnosed when the buzzing in his left ear, as satisfying at first as a white-noise machine, changed to clangorous and impatient bangs that jolted him upright several times in the night. The following morning, he would attribute the lengthening headaches to insomnia. The eventual diagnosis came a year later, following useless visits to a half-blind audiologist and a pair of gossipy naturalists.

His online search of the disease should have alarmed him, but he was not unduly worried. Because he only apportioned his life in decades, existing in expectation of what would follow rather than the events taking place around him, he anticipated he would be fine until he hit eighty. Both his parents had lived to their late seventies. He was reassured in this calculation by his family doctor, an ancient, plodding turtle of a man who also had never heard of an AVM and who spoke as if he doubted the existence of this ailment. ("Now spondylitis, there's a disease for you . . . twists you up like a duck's penis.")

This obsessive measuring of his life gradually drove away his few acquaintances. He had correctly anticipated he would be divorced in his forties, and in the months following the event, he felt unexpectedly liberated. He harboured no ill will towards his ex but he misjudged his bleak freedom; apart from a nine-month phase of drunken promiscuity, what followed was a sustained and involuntary celibacy that left him both damp and dry. In the meantime, his ex secured the interests of several successful men. He got dribbles of her social life from his children when they still visited. Once when his son asked him if he would remarry, he replied without thinking, "In a few years." He didn't mention the number fifty, but that was what he had in mind.

He visited art supply shops and bought paints, canvasses, and an easel. He also purchased a machine called Total Gym on which he had seen a remarkably preserved Chuck Norris sliding around in an infomercial, he ordered two books on midlife dating, and he stocked his cupboard with shirts that were too slack on the chest and pants too tight at the waist by the time he hit fifty, four years later. One night, he tripped on the exercise machine and landed on the pile of unread books. He cursed Chuck Norris and the following morning he examined the nasty bruise on his forehead, loaded the machine and a few books into his Toyota and disgorged everything at a local Value Village. That was a singular act, and he was briefly energized by the casting away of items. Later that year he stopped visiting his children, who had grown from precocious and surly teenagers into indifferent adults.

Although he never saw this, his fifties marked the greatest break from the preceding decades. The isolation, which felt like tiny pebbles bubbling close to his skin, soon fitted him like a threadbare jacket. The world began to press less heavily on him and gradually he grew used to the narrow view outside his room. He began a pair of paintings to reflect this view: the twist of the maple during windy mornings, the declarations of the midday light on the roof opposite, the sluggish march of the seniors during cool evenings, the children limber and spastic on their way to school; the rapt closing of the day. Those children, who had certainly noticed him peeping from behind the blinds, had probably written him off as an old man nearing the end of his life and too feeble to step outside. But he was already planning for his sixties. He would collect a pension and discounts available to retirees he had seen with their stark smiles idling in the malls. He would tap into seniors' vacation deals to faraway places. The decade that began on a depressing note ended with him, as ever, looking forward.

The year he turned sixty, he reflected on the benefits of superannuation, adjusting and adding to the list he had compiled over the years, but because these items had already been pounded into place, he speculated, idly at first, on what the seventies would bring. Habit soon took over, and he started making little preparations here and there. He bought pyjamas and cotton shirts, which he left in their wrappings, and a plaid jacket for unspecified occasions. He borrowed books on enuresis and other inconveniences and reflected on redecorations of the condominium he was renting. Every so often, he brought out his pair of paintings and added a few strokes that reflected his mood. Blue and grey slashes on swathes of crimson.

Sometimes he sat on the park benches and studied the fixed expressions and gestures of men a decade older than him. Now and again, he was disturbed by the realization that their muddled looks of dull curiosity and helplessness gave them apelike appearances, but he concluded this was so because they had divested themselves of all worries. In the pharmacies, he trailed these men and bought impulse items like walking sticks, denture powder, Viagra, lap blankets, and board games he shifted to the back of his closet, next to the murals he temporarily fetched out to study at the beginning of each decade.

But about practical matters, such as finally finishing his paintings, medical checkups, making a will, considering an insurance policy, notching up his savings, reconciling with his children, he did nothing; and when he was brought down by a brain hemorrhage at sixty-four, eighteen months after his AVM diagnosis, his two children whom he had not seen for close to a decade and who did not know their father's ailment, sat impatiently in the solicitor's office and discovered that his legacy amounted to seventeen hundred dollars in a chequing account, a Toyota worth eleven hundred but parked for the last year, a computer estimated at two hundred and oils and brushes that came to the same amount. The solicitor's aide did not bother with the junk, assigning the figure of seventy-five dollars. The last items were the murals and the pair of unfinished paintings.

If he had been there, he would hardly have been surprised by the paucity of his material possessions, but he would have been bitterly pained by the solicitor's judgment of his art. "Of little or no value." For in his mind, this was to be his real legacy. He had no idea if this bequest to his children was brought about by the quiet drip of regret or an act of revenge.

During their first visit to the hospital, a stout nurse with comforting rolls of fat under her neck and at the back of her arms met them in the hall and said in a low voice, as if she were passing a secret, that there was no hope. They listened patiently as, her neck rippling as gently as a sinister pond, she went on about death being preferable to a massive stroke, so they were surprised when their father remained on life support for close to two months. "He's on his way out," the nurse reaffirmed each time she spotted the pair. "He's going to a better place, honey. That's all there is to it." Once she winked and added, "He's there already but he doesn't know it."

"Someone should tell him," his daughter said, but only to herself.

His children were practical in ways he would never have understood. They each insisted the other be the prime beneficiary. Both demurred, but there were no arguments either in the hospital or in his former apartment where they were asked by the solicitor to visit. So while he was still hooked up to the machines, on his way out as the nurse claimed, they casually scanned his belongings, not touching anything, not passing their fingers over any fabric, not straightening the murals in his closet, not examining the pair of paintings; not establishing any connection. They wanted to get away from his place with its strange, compressed odours and were relieved to be back in the hospital that smelled of antiseptic and new rubber. (Later, they donated the Toyota to the Kidney Foundation; the computer, the still-boxed shirts, and pyjamas to Goodwill. The trove of medication in their unopened bottles they discarded with other bits of junk he collected over the years. The art they left in the apartment for the super, a Macedonian who, for some reason, always kept his hands hidden.)

If they were looking for some secret that might be revealed by the rubble, some personality to the assorted items they viewed from a distance, they were disappointed. Not knowing of their father's forward glances, they assumed his hoarding was emblematic of all the old men who lived alone. They showed no signs of curiosity in any case. Maybe there was some lingering resentment to their indifference, but more likely, they had lost contact for too long and, against all odds, cobbled together their own lives. They were most successful in their chosen careers, accountancy, the profession also of their mother. (At an earlier time, their father had felt he, too, should have been an accountant instead of an artist, but he knew that was impractical because numbers confused him. For instance, although he was precise about his own ebbing life, he never recalled the exact ages of his children or their birthdays. Trivial details, mostly architectural oddities, he remembered intimately.)

For his children, the hospital visits and the disbursement of his belongings had a ritualistic feel; a solemnization that granted closure to an event that needed no such nudge. There was no mystery to him; nothing that in their minds might separate his life and impending death from those of other men in their mid-sixties. His former wife did not visit, but she gave them a card signed both by herself and her boyfriend that their daughter placed on a table on which there were peeled-off labels and latex gloves that made her think of shredded skin. The card contained six words: There are no endings, just beginnings.

The son thought the card was vaguely funny, given the situation. (Derived most certainly, he suspected, from the new-age nonsense his mother had retreated into over the last few years.) Once, he held up the card before his father with a smirk and his sister seemed annoyed, but only because she could not understand her brother's bleak humour. Never close, they had grown apart since the brother developed a way of looking at the world that tried to be droll but which, to her, was mean-spirited. Sometimes, she caught herself glancing from father to son.

As the days passed, the pair lost these bits of distinctiveness and grew equally bored and impatient. "Any day now," the nurse assured them. "He's close to exhausting his bag of tricks." She uttered the word, "*Thukdam*," and the daughter wondered if the woman was replicating the sound of suffocation.

The man on the bed with his frozen expression was a stranger, and they wished they could be somewhere else. The neurosurgeon, with his gentle beard and soft eyes, came in a few times. He noticed the indifference of the children, how their blank expressions matched that of his former patient—he already thought of him in this manner—and imagined it was shock. He spoke gently, pausing and thinking and murmuring that gave his words a kind of rustic gravity. The son likened his bearing to that of a weary roadside preacher; his daughter, that of an absent-minded gas station attendant.

Everyone wants to breeze forward, he told the pair. It's the order of things. Children imagine themselves as limber teenagers. Teenagers fantasize about adult perks like marriage and a stable job. Looking ahead to children and all that. But at some stage, maybe the point just past middle age, the cogs slow and the projector whirs backward to times of health and irresponsibility and innocence. In your father's case, the mechanism got jammed, and he was trapped in the chaos of constant motion. He smiled his gentle smile. Well, in some ways, it's a better alternative to constantly nourishing the past with idealized events, hankering back to times of vitality, wouldn't you say? The neurosurgeon's eyes crinkled with his smile and the son wondered how often he had unleashed this benign pose on grieving relatives.

The father had confessed this to the neurosurgeon during his final visits in an almost argumentative manner, insisting the diagnosis was faulty. His chronology had already been laid out; the timeline set. The neurosurgeon realized his patient had slipped into the familiar attitude of preparing for a good life rather than an adequate death.

During their father's last week, the neurosurgeon spoke of Glasgow scales and about the thalamus and hypothalamus and basal ganglia and fronto-temporo-parietal networks. His voice was so gentle he could have been referring to houseboats gently ruffled by an ocean breeze. And that was what the son was thinking of during the conversation, the trip he planned and saved for close to a year. The description of the brain system made the daughter think of flowers, purplish and heavy with dew. She held on to these images whenever the surgeon retreated into his gobbledegook. The day he remarked that everyone now wanted to live to a hundred, deluded by newspaper articles about octogenarian cyclists and marathon runners, the daughter was imagining the dark-plum shades of a clematis.

She missed the following visit, and the brother experienced a vague twinge of resentment at her absence. What if he was forced into some decision? The neurosurgeon, too, was disappointed by the sister's absence. His medical jargon was not a means of impressing the pair; a choice had to be made soon. Before he left, he told the son, "Appearances can be deceiving. Your father, to all intents and purposes, is brain dead."

During that final week, while he was hooked up, the father's mind—or maybe the vestiges of his consciousness—wandered sometimes to the self-imposed junctures of his life but perhaps because of the anesthesia or because his synapses had begun to misfire, the brain turning on itself, the neat demarcations scattered and for the first time, he saw episodes rather than decades. The latter view had been highlighted by events, but the former forced him to see individuals. What he glimpsed weren't peaceful faces wreathed by light but a crowd lurching from a foggy valley.

He was frightened by their implacable advance, but the segment of his brain still performing, determined that these visions possessed the tenor of a nightmare. And so he waited for the end of the night.

The functioning fragments of his mind clung mostly to the nights and darkness. He dreamed of all the nights he sat alone in his bedroom outfitted with a king-size bed under which there were electronic items—radios, video players, a camera, a fax machine, all dusty and entangled with a mess of electrical cords. During those nights that always carried the dull odour of some prior celebration, the details of which he could never recall, he would finish his wine and imagine his children's sour surprise following the valuation of his paintings. These rare occasions were the only times he thought of his former family, for in the same way he trained himself to look forward, he also learned to forget segments of the past. Now, all that he shuttered were thrown up.

Two nights before he stopped dreaming, his babbling brain retrieved washed-out slivers of his past years. There were no recognizable faces this time, no personal experiences, and in fact, the events seemed to take place some distance away. The combined effect was not unlike a vague disquisition of a familiar but tiring project. But he sensed there was a narrative into which he was included. The night before his death, some pieces appeared to float towards each other, never really touching but creating a plausible memory.

He saw himself in the centre of the room into which he barricaded himself for more than two decades. The light from the upturned slat on the blind shone on the phone and the area above his easel, the illuminated dust seeming almost stationary above the pair of paintings. In one, a room appeared to be submerged with floating bodies and furniture, but when he held the painting upside down, the scene shifted to a shipwreck with jetsam and prone bodies on the ocean floor. The other painting depicted a scene bristling with silky flowers and mellow waves of cane-like grass. At one corner was a man strapped to a sugar windmill and at the other corner, behind the flowers and camouflaged by their green clothes, were two children peeping out. They were looking not at the man on the windmill but at tear-shaped leaves harassing the sky.

The former painting, spare and surreal, possessed a formality that seemed alien to him; the latter, garish and colourful, evoked the flavour of his muralist experience. He may have been surprised—if that function were still available—that his last thought was of his pair of paintings, the colours so fluid the details of one appeared to be leaking into the other. In this final recollection, something seemed to be forming, something new, and he guessed, remarkable. The details of the paintings were coalescing; the aspect of one was attaching to the other.

His son was not there that night but he had given his permission to disconnect their father and the nurse watching the tremors on her patient's fingers, the vein throbbing on his neck, the stifled breath placed her heavy hand on the daughter's shoulder. "He's travelling now," she said. The daughter imagined her brother's reaction to the nurse's odd description and felt a little smile tickling her lips. She pressed her fingers against her mouth. The nurse patted her shoulder. She was used to death, and she whispered, "Just a while again."

The daughter tried to recall the foreign word the nurse had spoken. It sounded like the impatient drip of water in a tubular cave.

A Parade of Ghosts

One evening, just after supper, I heard three evenly spaced knocks on my front door. It was too late for the sales reps who usually interrupted the evenings with their accented warnings of mites and dander only their devices could banish. At first glance, he matched the profile, but the lanky, bespectacled man standing before me, his hands folded against his back and his head bent like a bird appraising its situation, did not possess the jittery desperation I had spotted in the reps. Besides, he was wearing a purple cowl scarf. He peered into the open door. "Is that brother Monk I hear?"

"Yes. I listen to jazz when I am,"—I stressed the words—"reading quietly."

His lopsided smile matched the angle of his beret and I felt that within his haggard frame was the heart of a *sagaboy*. "I will get to the point. I am looking for a place to rent. Short-term. Six months to a year."

I began to explain that I had not advertised to rent a room, but he cut me off to ask if I was from an island. He stepped back and pushed up his enormous glasses. "You have the look, brother," he said. "Unmistakeably." He must have noticed my confusion because he added, "A tamed wildman dreaming of his lost wildness. Yes, yes. I see that in myself at the end of autumn when I am walking through the garden at Queens Quay. You wouldn't believe it, but on those chilly evenings, I hear the hoots of distant birds, the grebes and kestrels serenading me from the wildflower meadows. I hear other faraway-faraway melodies too." I could see his magnified eyes dancing behind his thick lenses as he sang Michel Jonasz's, "I'm Leaving Home, Mama." I was caught off-guard by his rendition, but his voice was low and melodious. I mentioned this and he revealed that he had trained as a radio announcer before he arrived in Canada. "We had a Rediffusion unit that could pick up the BBC and most of Europe. Radio Prague. I wrote a long letter to them detailing the pleasure they brought nightly to this country boy who lived in a thatched house with a mud floor. No electricity and no running water." His little nostalgic drift must have reminded him of his mission because he shifted a bit to gaze into the apartment. "Two bedrooms?"

"Yes, but very tiny—"

"I am not complaining. I am no longer the bon vivant of days gone by." He swished his wrist in an unexpectedly feminine manner. "My needs are simple. Can I take a brief look?"

As we walked through my apartment, I felt I had been pressured into this open-house and tried to think of a polite way to get rid of him. "Rather small, as I mentioned."

He had stopped before my bookcase and was sniffing the old Penguin and Fontana titles.

He plucked out a book and cradled it against his chest. "Ah, Galeano," he said, opening the book delicately and reading, "'The best language is silence. We live in a time of a terrible inflation of words, and it is worse than the inflation of money.' I hear you, brother. I hear you." He turned to me. "You have a marvellous selection here."

"I used to be a librarian. Retired last year from the—"

"I hope you didn't filch these books." He tipped back his head and emitted an asthmatic whine. "Forgive my laughter. I am a joker by nature." He replaced the book and stooped to look at the lower shelf. "I can see we will have many nights of erudite conversations."

"About that—"

He withdrew his wallet and handed me a gold embossed card with the name *Mr Rei Gouti. Soulsearcher.* While I was deliberating the name, he fiddled about in his wallet and brought out a folded cheque. "Can I borrow a pen? Oh, I think I have one here." He poked into the satchel round his waist. "My portable workstation. I am going to add two hundred more than I intended. Do you know why?" He scratched and scribbled on the cheque.

I wanted to say it was immaterial, but I was also curious as to the adjustment, so I shrugged.

He cocked an index finger and began tapping the spines of the books. "This is why. A man should not only pay for space but pleasure. When can I move in? The end of the month would be convenient for me."

That evening, I had one of those conversations with myself that I'd hoped would never return. "You are a jackass," I told myself. "People will nibble you down until you have nothing left. That is why you is a blasted sixty-year-old man with no wife, no children, no friends, no anything. Mister Rei Gouti! A fake name for sure." I heard knocking on the common wall of the living room and shouted, "Sorry, sorry. It's the TV. I will turn it down." The next-door tenant was a Portuguese mechanic who worked at night and slept in the day. He had moved in eight months earlier and his first words to me, delivered as a warning, were, "Rosa is naturally friendly, like all Brazilians. That's all there is to it. *Tu entendes*?" Rosa, either his wife or girlfriend, was a tall, buxom woman employed at a long-term care home, and although she walked and dressed quite provocatively, she was anything but friendly.

I was observing her retrieve a grocery bag from her car when a van pulled up. It was exactly seven days following Mr Gouti's visit and even though he had mentioned "just a few odds and ends," he and the driver proceeded to stack about twenty cardboard boxes on the driveway. I watched with some alarm as he walked across to Rosa, who with the two grocery bags in her hands, was surveying the disgorging. I couldn't hear their conversation over the van's engine, but he touched his beret and saluted before he returned to help the driver.

"That's a fair bit of stuff you have here." I gazed at the boxes we had taken into the small room.

"I have shrunk the dimensions of my possessions to fit into a single room. Mostly books and records." He flipped the lid of a box. "Ah, Baldwin, my old friend. I trust the journey did not upset you." He extracted another hardcover. "I placed you next to Ousmane Sembene. What were you two whispering about? Was it about the wedding night's impotence?" He shook his head sadly and read a passage, "'However long it stays in the river, the tree trunk will never turn into a crocodile.'" He gazed at the book's cover. He withdrew another book and spoke in a cajoling manner to the writer. This went on for a while. I suspected he was showing off, so I told him I had some work to do and returned to my room. It was mid-afternoon, and I dozed off.

When I got up three hours or so later, he was in my living room recliner. "I am sorry to have commandeered your lounger, my good friend." He stood up, and I saw he was as formally dressed as at our first meeting, with his stylish scarf and his long-sleeve shirt buttoned at the cuffs and the collar. On his head was his beret, on his feet a pair of navy socks, and in one hand a bottle of Douro wine. While we were sipping the wine, he showed me what he had unpacked. A banjo atop a pile of clothes on the bed, heaps of books at the foot, and three rows of LPs pushed next to a phonograph he had set against the wall. The two old fans on the coffee table looked like the propellers of vintage airplanes. "Not much, as I said. Just the markers that I carry around hither and thither. I give away a fair proportion with every move." As he packed his stuff, he asked, "Do you know that the banjo originated in Africa?" He began to sing, "'I'm a natural-born drifter, baby, I'm going from town to town, baby.'" He winked and said, "I hear you, Brother Hooker."

There was something unsettling about his insertion of songs in our conversations, the BBC-accented quotes, his buttoned-up shirt, his rakishly set beret, and for some reason, his two old fans. I regretted not cashing his cheques earlier in the week. "You mentioned a radio announcer's ambition," I told him.

"Sadly, it came to naught, brother. It was not to be."

"And so?"

"And so. The eternal question. What must we do next? If truth be told, I prefer to stay in the moment."

"In the meantime, though, we must all live."

"Well said. Yes, yes, yes. I must concede."

"All the books here . . . were you an educator of some kind? A high school teacher maybe."

He glanced at me with a measure of feigned surprise. "You have hit the nail on the head."

"Were you?"

After a while, he said, "Yes. Let's agree to not disagree on that."

In the night I heard his creaky fan intermittently drowned out by his phonograph scratching out old Bossa Nova and Bluegrass songs and tunes from the early nineties that I vaguely remembered. I wondered if the mechanic next door could hear them, though his room was on the opposite end. I fell asleep to Buffy

Sainte-Marie's, "I'm Going Home." It was the favourite song of the woman who had shared my apartment for more than a decade before moving back, two years earlier, to Nova Scotia.

The next morning, Mr Gouti came out of the washroom fully dressed and I asked if he was going out. "I may poke around later, but at the moment I shall amble around in the Hindu Kush. Thence, the Iron Rooster all the way to Tibet. Tomorrow I will set my sights on Patagonia. And for that, *compadre*, I need your Wi-Fi password." After I wrote the password, he said in a lugubrious voice, "I am a static traveller, you know. A nomad forever held in stasis."

He was held in stasis the entire morning on my recliner. I emerged from my bedroom a few times to reheat the kettle, and each time without looking up from his book, he waved with his buttoned-up wrist. By midday, though, he had disappeared and I reclaimed my recliner, where I fell asleep after lunch. I awoke at 3:30, the time Rosa usually returned from her afternoon jogs in her yoga pants, and when I peered through the front window, I saw Mr Gouti walking with her towards the driveway. I hastened to the recliner and when he entered, I asked if he had a pleasant stroll.

He adjusted the tilt of his beret and patted the curly hair at the sides. "Yes, yes yes. It is an interesting neighbourhood. If I were a decade younger, I would have planted my flag." He went to the fridge to unpack his groceries, humming cheerfully.

He disappeared into his room, and a few minutes later, I heard a banjo. I couldn't determine if it was from one of his LPs or if he was himself strumming. I am not a paranoid man by any means, but that afternoon I speculated anew about Mr Gouti. Did he know Rosa previously and was his appearance at my door an attempt to get close to her? And what was that talk about planting his flag? But he seemed my age, old enough to be Rosa's father. Then it struck me: what if he was? Assuming his Mister Rei Gouti name—which he pronounced as Mystery Agouti—was not fabricated, it was slippery enough to have originated from any continent. The same with his stained-cedar colouring. Moreover, I had never seen him without his beret and the thick glasses that disrupted the contours of his face. He could be anyone. From anywhere.

Early the next morning, from my room, I heard drumming on my chopping board. When Mr Gouti saw me, he said, "Today my friend, you are going to have a feast. Spicy f-o-u-l." He launched into a tune and I saw his Adam's Apple jumping up and down. "I'm a schemer with an eye for a show / It's my imagination when I get low. And the truth is I don't think I'll ever go." Sandy Denny, he informed me over the flow of the kitchen tap. Soon he began to wave the pot spoon and began a jerky dance. It was a sight, with his beret and thick glasses and buttoned-up shirt—he looked like a goose-stepping giraffe. Finally, he poured what seemed to be a mix of beans and pepper and garlic on a slice of pita bread. I took a tentative bite. "It's tasty."

"Indeed. It's a special Ethiopian dish I've augmented with my special juices."

I almost spat out the morsel. He talked about a taxi driver from Ethiopia, a learned man, a poet in his homeland who had been forced now to obey the commands of drunken revellers each night. The driver recalled idyllic scenes of Canada he had viewed in magazines back home and was saddened by the brutes who descended in his taxi, whom he saw in their uniforms at the street corners, striding inside the glass buildings. None were interested in him. One night he had to drop off a group of young writers at Harbourfront. They requested he return in two hours. Instead of driving around looking for fares, he parked. As he walked through the Allemande and the Courante, his worries fell away. He returned there each night after his shift. Then he started exploring similar places. Ashbridges Bay. The Humber River. He grew to know various shrubs and flowers he saw. Even the weeds. He gave them names from his boyhood and spoke to them. And they listened to the story of his life, the man he thought he would be, the struggle to become that man, and the eventual outcome. "You can guess the rest."

My narrator seemed to be waiting, so I asked, "He recovered the country he had imagined?"

"He invented it, brother." He got up and removed the plates. "He invented the country he had imagined."

"Did you know this driver?"

Mr Gouti began to scratch the back of his neck. "One night he told me I was the first person to show any interest in him. During my years as an extra, I travelled regularly with him. And others with similar stories. From Afghanistan. Pakistan. Somalia. Guyana."

"So you worked as an extra too? Was that before you were a teacher?"

"It's all in the past, brother. It's all in the past." He glanced at his watch. "Now I must tend to other matters. I keep a steady routine."

A few minutes later, I heard him whispering and giggling in his room. But he was right about his routine. Each day seemed to repeat the last. Whispered telephone conversations, departure around lunchtime, and reappearance with Rosa in the afternoon. Then there would be a few hours of silence but for the groaning of his fan and, late in the night, music.

The only variations were at breakfast: each morning he prepared a meal from a different country, and each morning he paired the cuisine with a story of someone who had arrived from the meal's point of origin. One morning, after a meal of eggs and tomato sauce and pepper that he referred to as *shakshuka*, he told me of a factory worker who dreamed of becoming a writer while he daily stacked cases of fruit juice on a conveyer belt. He signed up for a writing class run by a middle-aged man with a big floppy grin. After a week, he submitted a story based on his interactions with the Eastern European supervisor at the factory. It was panned by the instructor, who described it as "an artifice of grievances and resentments." The same thing happened with his second and third stories. He would have dropped out if he had not formed a promising friendship with a young woman from Estonia whose stories the instructor held up as "models of precision and sensitivity." One evening, he revealed his intentions to that writer, who always had this restful look, as if her head was nestled against a wall. She put her hand on his shoulder near his throat and suggested that as an experiment they should exchange stories for their next assignment and submit them using each other's names. They had been drinking, and he readily agreed. The following week he listened as the instructor looking squarely at him tore apart the woman's submission and then praise his as "burning with a controlled luminescence."

"He must have been relieved," I said to Mr Gouti during his moment of silence.

"Yes. He saw the world as it was. He never wrote another word again."

As I listened to his accounts of the farmworker from Barbados, the refugee from Sri Lanka, the Chilean who had overstayed his temporary work visa, the security guard from Trinidad, my interest in his relationship with Rosa was displaced by something much more intriguing.

I couldn't come out and ask him outright if he was relating aspects of his life; instead, I tried to engage him in conversations to allow him the opportunity for confession. All his stories were about set-upon men confronted with a moment of anguished clarity. The accounts were not unduly pessimistic, each of these characters—seeing the world as it was—was now better prepared for what might lie ahead.

But Mr Gouti parried all my inquiries, and he skillfully turned the questions back to me. He asked about a nineteenth-century painting of a black family trudging along with a cartload of goods and I told him that the Robert Petley piece had been left behind by a woman who once lived here. I noticed the curiosity on his face and explained that we worked together in the library and she had moved back to Whitney Pier in Nova Scotia. I didn't bother mentioning we had planned the move together, but I had chickened out at the last minute. Another day, he inquired about the book he had spotted during his first visit. Galeano. I told him that while in the library I had been focused on my job, I had also been curious about the men and women who regularly borrowed these obscure books. I had vowed I would do the same once I retired. But I would choose books from my slice of the world. Flora Tristan. Wilson Harris. Samuel Selvon. Alejo Carpentier. I soon discovered these authors were all beyond me, as I told Mr Gouti. He said on that first day he had mistaken me with my white beard and tousled hair and absentminded appearance for a writer. I shook my head and said that while I could spot anomalies, I did not possess any desire to change the world. I just wanted my little spot.

He scratched the back of his palms, watching the blue veins fatten and ripple. "That day I first appeared before you. I had already knocked on a dozen doors. And the minute you walked out, I thought I had found my sanctuary. Thelonious Monk. The book in your hand." He uttered this in a reflective manner as if considering his choice. Then he turned around and went into his room. Later I heard Lighthouse's "Thoughts of Moving On," streaming from his room.

That night I awoke from an uneasy dream of being mocked during my retirement ceremony at the Toronto Library. The sheet was around my feet and I had a sense of being watched. When I sat up to retrieve the sheet, I saw the silhouette of a figure against the door. I froze. The light streaming from the adjoining building was dim, but the figure was tall and undeniably naked. Before I had the opportunity to say or do anything, it had turned and left. The intruder's back seemed excessively hairy, like an animal's pelt. I recalled a charcoal drawing of Brer Anancy. I quickly got up and locked the door, and as an added precaution, I jammed a chair against the doorknob. I couldn't sleep after that and for the rest of the night, I was by the window looking down, my cellphone in my hand.

I emerged from my room at seven. It was the time Mr Gouti would be in the kitchen preparing one of his international meals, but I saw him sitting, his hands clasped before him on the table. Perhaps he is mulling over an apology, I thought, but the minute he saw me he sprang up and disappeared into his room. I considered knocking and demanding an explanation, but increasingly I grew unsure: the nakedness, the furlike back, the swift retreat, all had the tenor of a dream. I went to my recliner, and I heard him playing, "We are going softly now." It was a song by the band, The Broken Reed; I had not heard it since the mid-seventies, soon after I arrived in Canada.

It was in the early afternoon that he emerged. "Going for your afternoon stroll with Rosa?" I blurted.

It was a moment before he replied. "You have been paying attention." He looked at the front window. "Do you know how I first met her? It was on your driveway. I enquired where she was from and when she said Brazil, I inquired if she was The Girl from Ipanema. It's a Brazilian song." Then he grew silent and turned to face me.

"You have something on your mind?" I asked.

"There was a matter I wanted to discuss with you."

"Yes?"

"It's of no consequence now. I have made up my mind." He began to scratch his wrists. "Psoriasis. I try to keep my extremities covered so as not to alarm anyone. It's only in the nights that I completely free myself. I hope the humidity in Thailand helps."

"Thailand?"

"Yes. It was what I wanted to discuss." He mentioned he had met a Thai woman through some online chat site and she had invited him to her place just outside Bangkok. He described her house as surrounded by chrysanthemums and honeysuckles and a path at the back, lined with trees he referred to as golden showers, that led to a Buddhist temple.

"Did she describe these things?"

He must have seen my skepticism, because he said, "We people never have complete stories. We have episodes and installments but never a sense of fulfilment at the end. No sense the journey is completed. But we can't give up. We must push on." He revealed that he planned on leaving in two weeks and that he would pay in advance for the next three months. "If by then I do not return, you can dispose of the books and everything else. The records I will take. They have followed me wherever I go." The next few days, while he packed away his stuff and the gifts he had bought, he was in an extraordinarily good mood, singing, "Hit the Road Jack."

I must admit that I missed Mr Gouti more than I had expected. The morning conversations and the music streaming out from his room and my introduction to singers like Sister Rosetta Tharpe and Blind Lemon Jefferson and Portia White from Nova Scotia and Ahmad Zahir, the Afghan Elvis. Perhaps he, too, missed our little chats because every weekend he would WhatsApp me. He seemed to enjoy showing me images of the woman he was with, who had a chubby and pleasant face, and the flowers and the strangely named tree leading to the temple. He said that finally he had made a practical decision, as this remote village was the perfect place to be during the coronavirus pandemic, which had been barely newsworthy when he departed but had grown into a menace in the months since. I relayed news of all the measures that had been instituted here, belatedly, in the opinion of many commentators. Then one weekend, no call. Instead, there was a photograph of him with his beret and a cotton shirt. He was not looking at the camera but gazing at the guitar in his hands. The next weekend, there were no photographs or calls. I tried calling several times, but there was no response.

Two months following his departure, I put on my mask for a grocery run. Rosa was outside her doorway and the minute she spotted me, she came across. She had what seemed to be a newspaper clipping folded inside plastic. She returned to her apartment, and I placed the clipping in my mailbox. When I returned from the grocery, I retrieved it and, because I was cautious about handling plastic, I took it to Mr Gouti's room. He had taken all his LPs but for one, *We Are Going Softly Now*. I felt he had left it there especially for me.

I put it on the phonograph and I reread the clipping. "There are unconfirmed reports that a member of the Toronto jazz band, The Broken Reed, briefly popular during the 70s, has passed away from coronavirus in Thailand. The deceased, whose identity has been withheld as per the request of his fiancée, was reported to have lived an itinerant life following the breakup of the band. He never completely disappeared though, as there were sightings of him at various protests in the city."

I want to believe the deceased was not Mr Gouti. I prefer to imagine him sitting in the Buddhist temple, the singing bowls creating a harmonizing backdrop to his melancholic song. "The rain has stopped, the lights are lost / Going softly now, a parade of ghosts."

The Question

I want to describe a late-life shift you never got to experience. As we get older, our gazes shorten and in these rare moments when we breach our reduced view, we are astonished at how much the world changed when we were not looking. Sometimes, we blame others for what we see and sometimes ourselves. Ever since our grandson went missing, the only question on my mind was whether *he* knew more than he was letting on. They were as close as a father could get to his teenage son. But old men like myself, we make the world simple. Besides, as you know, I was never any good at stepping into the paths of others. Even those who share our blood. What would I say to this man who, if you spotted him now, would remind you of myself thirty years ago? Should I tell him he was a better father than I?

But curiosity, when it is squeezed, grows sharper. So I put myself in his path during his evening walks which he has kept up. One evening I almost told him, *You stay away from me, you are repeating my life. Look at how you too walk alone.* I must tell you it was surprising he could still manage a routine but the minute he spots me his feet get lighter. A few times I spotted a slight weakening, but this was my optimism more than anything else. The only thing I know for sure is that my sympathy is like acid to him.

Seven years ago, when his wife packed her belongings and left, I told him, "It's not too late. Work out whatever it is. The boy needs a mother. Give it a try." I saw the reproach in his eyes and added, "It's not the same, you know. Your mother had to work two jobs. It's how we survived."

I would have liked to tell him of our early struggles to make a life here, but he cut me off. "You . . . " I knew he was deciding what to say. In the end, he made his usual move. He walked away. For seven years it's all he has done. Now his son has repeated the pattern. Or maybe the pattern has changed. I don't know, because I have been cut off from everything.

This running away. This escaping. Maybe it's in our blood. Two generations ago, I slipped away from my parents, my country, my war, and never looked back. But I took my new wife. My love. My saviour. *Your slave.* Did he actually use those words? It does not matter; I saw it in his eyes. Now there's nothing there.

As I have done many times, I turn to my sole companion, our garden. Whether it's therapy or desperation, I do not know.

It's the end of winter now. You were always energized during this period, but me, I used to see life sucked out of the clematis vines we pruned to arch over the backyard gate. The strawberries and bee balm got reduced to brittle sticks. We were dissimilar in looks yet we were a perfect match. I think you would like the gardens on adjoining properties. They are decorated with solar lights of every shape and colour. At night they get transformed into glittering . . . what's the word? . . . palisades. I used to wonder what the raccoons and insects make of this decoration of the nights. A few evenings ago, I observed a squirrel flattening itself against a branch of the crab apple. Poor guy is suffering, I thought. Or poor lady. But soon they will all be out, the jays and the lone woodpecker that always sets about her task impressively.

I remember you in this manner. Tending the garden. Digging the soil. Stationing the cuttings you nurtured indoors. Refilling the holes with sheep manure. Punching the six-inch supporting stakes into the ground. Some of my most pleasant memories are of you in the backyard. I recall your joy when the roots took hold and the first buds appeared. I will tell you something I had been too shy to mention before. One evening I spotted you from the window. You were bunching a spreading lavender, and I hurried down the stairs. But you were so engaged in your act that I just halted at the door. Just watching you. Hair falling over your eyes. That was three or four months before your early retirement. I felt you, too, were thinking of the time when, free of your eight-to-four job, you could finally relax in your garden.

We make all these plans. We wait so long. We attend to every tiny detail, but life always steps in. When you were diagnosed with cancer eight months following your retirement, I tended the garden with as much care as you had. Sometimes I believed you would be cured if I devoted myself to your plants. You passed away fourteen months later, and I felt betrayed. I avoided the backyard. The weeds grew wild. The redbuds and bloodroots and your favourite, the fragrant daphne with its intermingled aromas were lost in the maze of feather wheatgrass. Above, the crab apple and willow seemed to be consoling each other. I didn't care one bit. I blamed your plants. But the plants managed. And two springs after your death, I spotted flowers peeping out, soft and panicky as abandoned babies. I considered hiring a gardener but I couldn't stand the thought of thick dirt-crusted fingers replacing your plants with delicate little annuals. You never liked annuals. They die too easily, you once said. I want a plant that grows like a child. One I can nurture and nourish.

You never saw your grandson and I wonder what you would have made of his disappearance. I feel everything may have been different if you were still here. These useless speculations dig deep under the skin but you had a way of quietly taking charge. Right from the beginning. It was you who decided I should return to university when we arrived here. You were a teacher back home, you insisted. Nothing I said changed your decision. In the nights, while I was poring over my essays you saw to our son's homework. You were so diligent that I remarked once, "We should exchange jobs." Do you remember how you took it as a joke and smiled? You may have missed our young son gazing expectantly at us. That expression changed over the years from expectation to annoyance. And finally, to disregard.

A week following our grandson's disappearance, I mentioned I had not seen the boy recently. He muttered something about a spring camp. I asked about the camp's location and the activities. His silence seemed to be saying: Leave me alone. I am no longer the little boy you tried to bamboozle with your optimism. I am not like you. I tried to be a real father.

He was, you know. I remember how he'd look bright when he was with the boy. Cheerful. During their backyard basketball and their walks. I admired the way he stepped up, playing both mother and father. As you know, we are from a part of the world where the bond between father and son is not shown as open affection as in this country but by layers of prohibitions and injunctions. So, I thought the boy would turn out okay. He would return the friendship in small ways. No two relationships are similar, I thought; no two years alike. I held hope.

This year the squirrels are out in full force, harassing the gladiolas and leaving the nibbled bulbs like beacons on my driveway. In my basement apartment—I moved there following your departure—I hear a woodpecker tapping away at a crab apple. In the nights, the taps seem like a distant cry for help. Soon, it will be a month since the boy's disappearance and I know he is in no camp. It's the middle of April, his second semester in college. The college his father attended and the one his grandfather taught until his retirement. I was the only foreigner on the staff at the time and among the students there were just a handful from other places. They would look at me with shy interest. If they had ever asked why I never returned their curious glances, I would have said that in this new land we were just like everyone else. No favours asked, no favours granted. You felt my approach was harsh and I should understand the deep hankering for familiarity.

Everything's changed now. The city has changed. When we bought this house thirty-three years ago, there were only boxy warehouses and abandoned lots around. Now the place is congested with high-rises and two-lot mansions. The once-empty plots are bristling with mosques and temples and gurudwaras. People become more devout, it seems, when they are pulled away from their gods. I imagine their morning prayers, "Hey, Father. Look around. We have not forgotten you." You hated it when I made jokes about people's gods. Not everyone is so shameless, you would chastise me with your little smile.

Soon after his wife left. I told our son, "We have so much to be grateful for. The boy will be okay." I was thinking of his coming distress in raising his son as a single parent. But he pulled the boy closer to him. As if he were shielding him. He took him on trips to Algonquin and Manitoulin Island and they sometimes spent the entire week at some camp along Georgian Bay. I was never invited and in time I grew used to their absence. I was not offended. In fact, I was pleased that they went to these remote places where they would be alone with each other. The father is preparing the son, I thought. Teaching him about the unknown and the unexpected. Preparing him for life.

The lilacs are blooming. The panicles of purple put the other colours to shame. Yet it is the colour of mourning. I think of this when I enter the hospitals. I have visited every one in the city. St Mikes and Toronto Western and even those in Scarborough and North York. "He is eighteen years old," I told a nurse with lines of either impatience or overwork on her forehead. "Light brown like myself. Five foot seven. Or two or three inches taller." I move my hand to the tip of my head. Once I asked a young nurse, "Is there a ward for suicide patients? Maybe he's there. He has become withdrawn. Sleeps all day and on the computer all night."

The nurse rolled her eyes, an insolent gesture but one that comforted me. She seemed to be saying, He's a teenager. Get over it. They are all like that.

I could have told her of a conversation I had with the boy two years earlier when he was about sixteen and taking up with things I had left behind. Becoming critical and moody for no visible reason. Once I mentioned that we were fortunate to be in this country where we could be whatever we wanted. Really, grandpa? he asked, and I felt it was because the poor boy was still missing his mother. As I continued about how lucky we were, how some of my cousins had been killed by neighbours in the old country, he interrupted me. "There's nothing wrong with being killed by your own."

Nothing wrong? Your own? Where did he get these thoughts from? I sputtered out. And he told me, "We are different. I have nothing to be grateful for. I didn't ask to be born here."

So the relief brought about by the nurse did not last. Each night, I listened to news reports of gang warfare and accidents in high-rises and on the roads. Anything about the death of a young man with a foreign name. I scanned the newspapers too, and soon I began to widen my field because he could have gone to some other province. The only thing I got from this focus was the knowledge that the country has changed. Groups and associations demanding recognition. New terms like intersectionality and ethnic privileges. So much confidence!

But I had other things on my mind. I turned my attention to my son. Maybe I could get some clue about the boy's whereabouts, but he consistently ignored my attempts at conversation. Still, I wanted to believe that when he passed me in the early evenings kneeling before my plants, he knew my mind was not on gardening. A week earlier, I had asked if the boy had gone to his mother. "His mother is dead," he said with so much hate that I momentarily believed this was true. The following evening, he saw me waiting and said abruptly, "The trucks are here." Each year during spring the city truck deposits a load of topsoil and sheep manure at the corner of the street. I take longer now to tote the four or five buckets to the garden.

This midday while I was spreading the topsoil at the front, around the roses, I wondered: What's the use? Who am I leaving this for? Yesterday, I found out, at last, the answer to my question. It was the one I least expected. I had barely slept the previous night. Every two or three hours I would awaken and open our old album. The family portraits were taken at different times. Two faces in the first. Three in the second. Four in the third. Once, I imagined this extension was natural. Multiplying was the way of the world. Last night I missed you more than I ever did but I must carry on. This morning I dried my eyes and walked up the stairs. When I saw our son backing out from the garage, I tried to compose myself. He rolled down the window a few inches. I steadied my voice and told him, "It's not too late—"

"And I am late for work."

"Is there anything . . . " But he was already out of the driveway.

I wanted to tell him I knew what had happened to the boy. That it was not his fault. We could still bring him home by some means. In the evening, he spotted me waiting by the driveway and he drove around. I felt my knees weaken and for a moment I believed I would fall on the cobblestone border. If you had been there, I would have asked you, when does despair dip into disgust? But I have no allies in this fight. That same night I got up and gathered the photographs. I had no idea what to do with them so I placed each face down on the turntable next to my Zenith clock radio. I looked at the clock blinking the time until I dozed off. That had been happening with increasing frequency since I turned seventy, two years ago. I fought the regular downness. I took walks in the winter and fall. Tended your garden in spring. I tried to avoid my apartment as much as I could.

Now I feel as if I should just remain here and pretend I live in a happier time. Find comfort from the relics I have collected over the years. The turntable, our first big purchase, the fondue set, the decals from the first car we owned, the 1959 El Dorado, the mugs from our trip in the El Dorado to Niagara. Some you wouldn't know, like the photograph of uncles and cousins posing in their orchard. I had fetched the photographs from their creamy envelopes after your passing. Maybe I was looking for familiarity. Maybe. Now, these relatives seem to be lacquering the room with their frowns (as if they had expected this all along). At the side of my bed is the Zenith clock radio with carrying handles and dials that can only tune to the CBC programmes.

It was on the Zenith that I first learned of our grandson. The news had been broadcast between updated information on the flooding at Union Station and the gardening show you always listened to. It's strange that I remember more of the gardening host's advice that day about pruning than of the young man—nameless at the time—reported missing. Then, it was seen as an ordinary disappearance. (As if these events can ever be ordinary.) It was another two days before the pieces came together, strung from emails and telephone conversations and internet sites. As the CBC announcer mentioned the trio of teenagers who had left to fight a war they knew nothing about, I was astonished. Astonished that all these strands could be strung together by a journalist to create, or recreate, a complete life. I knew nothing of our grandson. But his life was out there, a strand here, a strand there, waiting to be woven.

Still. Still, I was sceptical. And hopeful and foolish. There had to be a mistake. The father had not raised his son to be this way. They took trips together. They were close. Then the video was broadcast, grainy and grey and I saw the boy I once knew, talking with an accent that was so pretentious and apish, I knew that this boy who once flinched at the sight of blood, was now capable of anything.

Today while I was pruning the roses, I almost snipped off my little finger. I pressed the injured digit and went inside to our medicine chest. While I was bandaging my finger, I thought of something. Small things are easy to deal with, not because they are small but because they float lightly and can attach themselves to restoring flecks and simply sail away. But some events resist redemption no matter how many times you turn and twist them. Did our son know all along? Was he just as astonished and confused? And—the question that lingers the longest—was he truly disappointed? I cannot understand his silence or his refusal to collapse under the weight of the betrayal set upon him. If betrayal it was.

How could he not know? The question haunts me. It has been in the news now for close to a week. I am certain everyone on the street knows by now. I am forced to wonder if our grandson really got his ideas from men thousands of miles away. At one time our teachers and guardians were men and women we knew and respected but now that special role can be fulfilled by a stranger with a computer. But maybe the boy's influence was local. Maybe right above my head.

I will reveal something you may not believe. For the first time since your death, I miss the old country. Do you remember the extended family gatherings? There would have been one of those. Relatives would have been summoned. The evening would be filled with shouting and pleading and advice freely given. When everything was finally resolved, there would be wine and food and songs. I know you would point out the inaccuracy of this picture. You would remind me that this picture belonged to a different time, that our village with its vineyards and orchards was now a rubble of boulders and smoke and dust. I know this is true. And I feel there is another truth I do not want to accept.

I try to recall if I ever painted a glorified picture for a little boy. Created a lost paradise needing a saviour. A superhero. My recollections of our conversations throw up no such descriptions. Yet, what if something had slipped out? A trivial description of a nectarine tree overlooking a ravine? The moonlit sky? The aroma of roasted lamb? It could have been anything.

Today the cops came. A woman and a man. I was in the front yard and pretended not to notice the car idling on the curb. I almost raised my shears in a friendly way but did not know how they would interpret that gesture. I continued with my pruning. They got out of their vehicle. The woman was short and a little stocky, and—please do not be offended—in her stature, she reminded me of you. The man was taller and his hands were long and twitchy. I assumed it was the woman who would be the good cop, but it was the man. The woman asked me to place the shears on the ground and when I straightened, the man asked if I had a bad back. His father in some small northern town had to retire from his farm because of his back. The woman asked how long I had been living here and if I was the father of the disappeared boy. I must have looked alarmed because she said, "You never know with some . . . "

During her pause, I tried to pack firmness into my voice. "I am the grandfather. And I have no idea where he is. Everything I know is from the news."

"Is there anyone at the back?" She walked to the back garden, and I knew at once they had been watching the house for days.

When she returned, I told the pair. "The father returns from work at five."

The man nodded and glanced down at his partner who was watching me carefully. They walked away abruptly, and I felt my temper rising. At first, I thought it was having to be put through this. Then I was angry at my quiet response. By the time our son pulled into the driveway four hours later, my anger found a more valid target.

I tried to walk off my bad temper. I noticed curtains shifting on some windows. A few men were on porches but no one offered a greeting. By the time I got back, I was breathing heavily. I repeated this pattern over the next two days. On the third day, our son came later than usual. When he got out of his car, I noticed a smudge of freshly cut grass on the toe of a shoe. It was close to seven, and I wanted to ask why he was so late. Instead, I said, "The police came earlier this week."

"The insects are out," he said, looking over my head at a climbing rose twirling around a trellis. I waited. "The insects are out," he repeated and walked to the doorway.

"Wait."

My momentary hesitation allowed him to say, "There are new bugs now. The warmer weather is bringing them here."

"The plants will be fine but—"

"You can't predict the nights," he said, stepping inside, and I was sick with myself. Here we were, small-talking about bugs and my plants. As if the boy were still next to him. As if nothing had happened.

Summer is almost gone. My grandson is still fighting his war. There have been a few newspaper articles lumping him with other young men. Some articles are scholarly, others are filled with fever. Occasionally, there are newspaper comments from neighbours. *They kept to themselves. Who would have imagined that someone from our quiet neighbourhood . . . but you never know, right? This place is changing too quickly. They are all the same.*

I have passed the stage where I worry about our neighbours. Once, I wondered if they saw me as the dangerous patriarch or as a tragic, ransacked figure.

I still have our plants. Most nights, I put on my sweater and I walk up the steps to the backyard garden. The moonlight seems to soften the leaves of the corydalis so they resemble carelessly painted versions of the medallions that hang from the stem of my reading lamp. You had made a necklace from the medallions I collected during my teaching days and those our young son had won when he was still interested in hurdles. I believe it was a Christmas gift, one of your last. On a postcard you had inscribed: *The only thing you own is time.* Time, yes. It has not unfolded the way I imagined. Maybe you were wrong in this. It is time that owns us. Frequently, I wonder how you would have handled this last year. What would you have said to our son about his recent decision to move elsewhere? You had chosen our house, negotiated the price, decided on the furniture, and planted the first garden. I was a bystander. I still am.

Sometimes I hear little snuffling sounds, a tiny animal creeping about, and at the same time, a click above me. Then I would glance up and notice smoke escaping the window and know our son is still awake. When I am in the garden, I still hold the frail hope that he will walk down the stairs and open the back door. The night holds the sort of soft coldness where secrets can be set out as neatly and in the same order as our dinner plates once, all four of them. So I wait, pretending I am looking beneath the leaves of the blue catmint for the little white eggs the aphids have left behind. I wait until the night chill grows unbearable and my expectation turns cold.

My dismay seems more streamlined in the night but by the morning, it is splintered. I listen to the morning host on CBC radio talking about the traffic snarl caused by some parade or exhibition. "If you are not going too far, it's better to walk," he advises. His co-host, chirpy a minute earlier, reminds him in a sombre voice about the upcoming interview with a mother whose son has been shot in a drive-by shooting. I turn up the volume on my way to the washroom. When I return, the mother is lamenting the loss of such a vibrant life. She lists some of his early accomplishments, cries, lists a couple more and cries again.

I feel she is blaming her boy's friends or the city itself but at the end of her interview, she says, "If I had only known it would end like this. If I had only known . . . "

I wait for the interviewer to ask her: What would you have done? What would you have done if you had known? I try to understand the woman's plea as if it could somehow provide answers to the issue closer to home. And I feel my anger returning, not because I disbelieve this woman but because her grief is so unsatisfactory and incomplete. Maybe it's just my mood.

It's early fall now and in the nights our garden is transformed. Fifty years earlier, I had been unprepared for the change of seasons and

I could never understand the devotion you lavished upon plants that would shrivel in a few months. So much effort and for what? If I close my eyes, I can hear the click of beetles on the stems and the dull gnawing of a small animal. I imagine I hear the shift of dirt and the crisp sound of tiny feet, and on the maple above, three settling flaps as if a blanket were being laid out for a nighttime picnic. I had seen a picture of this, of animals picnicking in a topsy-turvy field. But that would have been ages ago, in another country, where I imagined my life would follow the pattern prescribed for generations. I would not have known of the break in this pattern. The separation. The reshuffling of the past.

When I open my eyes, the sounds scatter and the fairy-tale image of picnicking animals is replaced with the knowledge of constant snipping and blighting. I pass my hand along a stalk and startle a leaf litter mantid out of its camouflage.

Senor Sewerpuss and Glamourgoat

Mr Herbert Bumphrey Wardle—not his real name—was a small, balding man with a soft belly that he thrust forward pugnaciously whenever he felt threatened. This was often the case; he viewed his life as composed of a series of near misses, and this notion of snatched opportunities roused him to bouts of brittle temper that were openly mocked by his coworkers at the newspaper. Each morning on his way to the office in Scarborough, he passed a homeless man whose friendliness he saw both as a trap and an assumption of kinship. On the day Mr Wardle was fired, the homeless man thrust out his palm, thumb and little finger touching as if he were about to issue a sorcerer's incantation and shouted after him, "Everything returns, master. Console yourself with that thought. Tell them Godbolt sent you."

"Tell Godbolt I don't fucking care," he muttered softly because he did not want to get into an argument.

That night, his insomnia was worse than usual. He got out from his closet a twelve-year-old unfinished manuscript, placed it on top of a stack of empty pizza boxes, and sat on his treacherous recliner watching a salesperson on his television who could either be thirty or eighty, selling a vibrating unit. He soon grew tired of waiting for the vendor to change his expression, a weird baby-like grin that never flickered during the entire time. Eventually, he turned on his old Dell desktop and typed "sugar tits." Now, though, he did not feel the familiar rush of pleasure because images of himself sprawled next to the Godbolt man kept popping up alongside the buxom women on his monitor. His old fear of being cast into the street, instigated by the tumultuous parting of his parents and gradually blunted by other anxieties, returned with a fury.

On the weekend following his termination, he was about to turn off his computer when he noticed an advertisement tucked away at the bottom of a gossipy news site, *ShitnStuff*, studded with infantile memes. "Looking for a writer. Can work remotely." He pushed aside his suspicion that the ad was aimed at one of the adult stars on the site and emailed his resume. Two days later, the publisher—just thinking of this designation gave him a headache—made contact. He was exactly as Mr Wardle had pictured him: thirtyish, with tiny malicious eyes and a beard that must have sprouted over the last month because it barely hid his pimply cheeks and the gap where a chin should have been. The man asked where he had heard about the job and Mr Wardle said it was from a site that parasitized headlines from real newspapers.

"Tell me about yourself."

"I have been a journalist for over twenty-five years and during that time I—"

"Not interested. What drives you? What's your passion?"

"I am working on a novel."

The publisher leaned forward and his spongy nose filled the screen. "Like everyone else. What's your pet peeve?"

"I dislike howlers," Mr Wardle said, a bit angrily.

"Monkeys? Expand."

"I am talking about the cacophony that surrounds us. The

constant blare of gossip and innuendo."

"So, you hear voices. I like it. If someone were to describe you in a sentence, what would they say?"

Mr Wardle thought of all the descriptions flung his way. His parents, before their separation, habitually referred to him as a sponge, his therapist had labelled him a seasoned hypochondriac, his old boss had branded him a misfit, and his one partner, a boozy social worker, routinely condemned him as a stingy gnome. "I cannot fathom the thoughts of others."

The publisher must have believed Mr Wardle was joking because he emitted a belchy one-note chuckle. "I will get back to you."

Mr Wardle supposed that was the end of it, but a few hours later he received an email from HotDiggityYo! that began with, "fyi pl see att article imo. nsfw." He didn't try to decode the email but went to the linked article, a YouTube compilation of increasingly dangerous pranks played by a young man on his willing girlfriend. Mr Wardle was intrigued as he watched clips of a tarantula thrown at the bound girl, a python let loose on her bed, shampoo replaced with red dye, a fake proposal, superglue on her toothbrush, and cling-wrap on the toilet seat. He waited for the girl to throw her boyfriend's bony ass out of the apartment, but once it was established that she had been filmed, she erupted into giggles. After an hour of viewing, Mr Wardle concluded that she deserved every bit of abuse. He sent a brief email to Mr Diggity. "What am I supposed to do with this?"

"Int pr roti," came the reply an hour later.

Internal procedure? Into prostitute? And roti? A quick online search showed it to be a kind of flatbread. He diverted into one of his saved sites, *Rubenesque Cubes*, before he emailed the editor who clarified that he wanted Mr Wardle to *interview the pair* and submit a *Record of Taped Interview*.

Mr Wardle, curious about the unhinged couple, decided against protesting. Besides, the girlfriend exhibited a feature his bookmarked sites typically referred to as a "peachy posterior." So, later in the day, he contacted the pair and explained that he was interviewing—he swallowed twice and forced out the word—for an e-zine. Halfway through the online interview, he realized he had misjudged the couple; they were even more shameless than he expected. To be certain, he returned to their YouTube videos, and he was surprised that he, and millions of others, had missed the way the girlfriend arched her back to thrust out her peachy posterior as she opened the fridge where her boyfriend was hiding, or her perfect hair and makeup while she slept, or the polished pitch of her little squeals of terror when she awoke to the python sprawled on her pillow. The miserable little fuckers, he thought. The girlfriend was into everything and the so-called pranks had all been staged. He submitted his unflattering article that night.

Mr Wardle was awakened by the pinging on his computer not long after. He dragged himself out of bed and signed on. The publisher's ghostly face appeared next to his HotDiggityYo! username. "You crazy, dog? These are among the top twenty YouTubers. If we publish this, I'm done. Fans will be down my gullet."

"I don't care about the fans or your gullet," Mr Wardle replied sleepily. "If their fans are so gullible, they deserve each other."

When the heavily edited article was published online, Mr Diggity emailed Mr Wardle. "Scroll down to comments. Clapback as expected."

Mr Wardle had never been called so many nasty names before, not even by the social worker he had shacked up with when his real journalism career was stable. Shiteater. Douchebag. Twat. Scrote. Dipstick. Abbreviations new to him. One commentator wrote, "Sewerpusses like you should DIAF!!!" He didn't know what DIAF meant or whether sewerpuss was a misspelling but he didn't care. He felt invigorated and following a foray into *Wenches on Benches*, he deleted his unsent letter of resignation.

His next article, which he submitted with the byline, Senor Sewerpuss, brought even more delightful insults. The focus this time was on an Influencer, a young man, clearly unhinged, who filmed himself screaming and crying and pushing back his bangs as he berated a host of genuine celebrities for what he viewed to be unforgivable infractions, like wearing mismatched swimsuits or choosing baby names he disapproved of. At first, Mr Wardle imagined a deliberate comedic structure to the hysterics, but he soon realized the performer was serious. And he was just as serious when he wrote that this young man should be immediately flung into an institution accompanied by his enablers.

The responses were magnificent. We know who you are! We will 4chan your doughy ass! KO your RBF! Following this piece, Mr Wardle felt like he was on a low-grade mission. He took special aim at their fans, whom he presented as roaches and gophers. (Names he borrowed from regular commenters) Mr Diggity simmered down when he discovered the agitated acolytes stampeded to his site not for elaborate articles about cellphone and wireless providers and cosplaying teens or convoluted DIY instructions but for Mr Wardle's columns. There were never any real rebuttals but rather insults like, "Senor Sewerpuss Totally Destroyed!" or "Epic Takedown!" For the same reason, Mr Diggity tolerated Mr Wardle's mocking of sites similar to his own.

It was easy for Mr Wardle to find them. They were emblazoned with headlines commanding you to read this article immediately or your life would be ruined and almost identical lists that determined if you were a psychopath, a missionary, or a child star. Mr Wardle was writing an article about a site crammed with articles like *Haikus to Recite to your Partner During Oral Sex* when Mr Diggity sent him a text that he ignored. A few minutes later, the publisher called on Zoom. "Something weird is happening. Crazy shit."

Mr Wardle listened with growing fascination. He never really expected much from the job; he knew the salary would be dog-shit, and it was, but for the first time in his forty-seven years, he was actually experiencing something close to satisfaction. Over the following days, he incrementally decreased his visits to online sites with bevies of lounging bosomy women. Mornings were no longer accompanied by the familiar sense of doom and his windows were not closed the entire day. He stopped turning his back on the other occupants of the elevator and once he experimented with a smile at a dwarfish old hag who clutched her ugly little dog tighter. One afternoon, he even flung a loonie at Godbolt, who impassively watched it rolling by.

The night his insomnia left him, he knew his new mood was not, as he had imagined, the joy of having all these online bullies clamouring for his head but witnessing the world rebalancing itself. He recalled the publisher of the newspaper where he had slaved his entire adult life explaining that he was writing for a "demographic no-zone" and that his replacement was a twenty-nine-year-old who "checked all the boxes." As Mr Wardle had gathered his possessions, the newspaper publisher said in his soft, clingy voice, "The world is changing. But there is a place for everyone. Even for you. You just have to find it."

Now the tables were turned. He was surprised by the ages of the celebrities who kept popping up in viral videos that usually involved an outlandish confession, a juvenile prank, or a mish-mash of alarming health advice and beauty regimens. He had typically confined himself to the corner of the internet populated by buxom women but he now saw influencers—a new term—running around, offering roses to the homeless and paying for their groceries, while recording their confused reactions. Briefly, he was fascinated—and alarmed—by this new world with no private spaces, where everyone wanted an audience, and by the public displays of pique and the absolute dread of "cancellation." At times, he wondered what might be the state of the world if, in the past, codes had been written by teenagers. But the fans! They seemed more unhinged than their idols. The last article he wrote had been titled *Shitrollers*.

So when Mr Diggity told him about influencers and YouTubers committing suicide, Mr Wardle assumed he was blaming him. But it soon emerged that the publisher wanted him to investigate this phenomenon. Mr Wardle suspected, at first, that it was all a big publicity stunt and the teenaged Influencers would soon pop up on the screens to talk about their traumas or insights, but a quick search showed that Mr Diggity was right. He felt a brief clench of sympathy when he read of the deaths from disease and wondered if it was the sense of impending extinction that caused these juveniles to seek some sort of immortality through their online junkets. But the sympathy melted as he came across others who died from running alongside trains or coddling pet pythons or taking selfies on the edges of cliffs. Five or six, he noticed, had been murdered by unamused relatives. Investigations are continuing, the police mentioned, and he concluded it would be wise to allow the authorities to finish their investigations.

Which left close to a dozen cases where death was caused by hanging, bullets, or overdose. He removed those who had overdosed, and the deaths were halved, leaving five young men and women who, at the height of their popularity, ended their lives. When he Googled their names, he was presented with mostly maniacal tributes compiled by their grieving fans. His attempts to contact relatives to separate exaggeration from fact were rebuffed with responses that ranged from threatening to reproachful. Have you no shame, one replied. Another sent a long email into which were interjected legal threats. Yet another responded to say, "Can't you parasites just leave us in peace now that Capricorn is dead and gone? All of you who hounded my beautiful child to her death. Get your own life now. She is gone." The email continued in this vein and he concurred with the woman he assumed was the girl's mother. So he replied to say that he agreed. He also pointed her to his early articles where he had excoriated these hangers-on.

Mr Wardle didn't expect the woman to reply, but soon he received a response. She ended by saying they could meet, but it would have to be face to face. He agreed at once, even though he had no idea where she lived and his meagre compensation at the e-zine did not cover trips. She emailed him the name of a pub in Oshawa, east of the city. The next day, he took the GO train to Oshawa and wished she had suggested a less crowded place. He scanned the crowd for someone who looked like she was grieving, a downcast, middle-aged single woman sitting by herself. The pub was filled with women who fit this description. An hour later, he left. When he got to his apartment, there was a message on his answering machine apologizing for not showing up and suggesting a meeting the following day at the same place and time.

That night, an old dream returned. A huge frog was clamped to his head taunting him with the voice of Arnold. "You are sissyboy. Ha ha. I am going to ram my fist into your stomach." It was two AM, and it was useless trying to get back to sleep. He attempted to finish an article requested by Mr Diggity on Vlogs—which he had assumed referred to some sort of sex toy—but his mind was elsewhere. When he stood by the window, he saw in the distance, Godbolt illuminated by the streetlamp, gazing up, his hands clasped.

All week, he got phone messages and, from the woman's voice, he formed an unflattering image. So when he eventually relented and agreed to meet her the following week, he was surprised when a curvaceous woman in her mid-forties with a generous jaw and an inviting lump of fat on her neck came to his table. She was dressed in faded jeans and a tightly stretched jersey and, from force of habit, he briefly assumed she was a prostitute.

"Are you the journalist?" She looked at him suspiciously as she pulled a chair. She had a pleasant tobacco odour and wore rings on several of her fingers. He noticed a couple of men in the pub glancing in their direction and felt the onlookers were puzzled about the pairing of an attractive woman with a short, overweight man with rumpled clothes and thinning hair. He recalled with some shame how a young woman from his apartment building had mistaken him for the janitor.

This woman had a disconcertingly direct gaze, but his discomfort eased as she spoke of her daughter, Capricorn, bullied relentlessly in school because of her appearance. He formed an image of an accompanying ugly father, but the woman began talking about raising a child as a single mom. "I used to have friends over." She glanced up and her big, slightly inflamed eyes softened.

"Why did you stop having your friends over?"

"Capricorn had enough problems as it was. Rejected by her father and at school. Her real life was online and she poured her heart out." She must have caught some look on his face, because she leaned back and drew her collar closer to her neck.

A man with a denim jacket and huge fingers clamped around a beer bottle was staring frankly in her direction. He tried to follow the onlooker's gaze and his eyes dropped on her breasts. They seemed mellow and cushiony, like those of the women from one of his saved sites, *Muffin-tops and Meatballs*. He lost concentration: she was saying something about her daughter. He caught the last sentence and asked her, "Turn out like you?"

"Yes, that's what I thought. That it was a phase Capricorn was passing through and she, too, would change." She formed a triangle with the index fingers and thumbs of both hands. He felt that this shapely woman had been starved of companionship for a long time and wished she would talk more about herself.

"Did your daughter mention what she thought about the men you brought over?"

"She didn't have to."

"Did she witness something?"

She glanced above her triangle and her gaze was so fierce he had to look away. She got up suddenly, her chair scraping the floor. "Are you coming?" When they were leaving the pub, he noticed the man with the denim jacket finishing his beer as if he intended to follow them. Outside, the woman lit a cigarette and inhaled deeply. She tipped her head and exhaled. "I picked up the habit once more when Capricorn . . . " She took another long drag. "I blame myself for encouraging her to create this other life. The public one. I still do."

She flicked the ash and regarded her cigarette. Mr Wardle regarded her breasts. She seemed to be waiting for him to say something. "You shouldn't," he began. He wasn't sure where he was going with this. All he knew was he wanted to comfort this woman who would soon lose her attractiveness. And maybe it was standing next to her, the sense of her crumbling, the odour of her sweat not entirely masked by the cold air; maybe it was all of these but he, whose last conversation with a woman was a brief query—"How much?"—found words.

And how the words flowed! He told her of all the enablers who tossed up and dragged down vulnerable children like her daughter. They were all parasites looking for weaknesses, voting down those who had fallen out of favour. The disfavoured deserved this for exposing their lives to perpetual scrutiny. But not your daughter, he added quickly. And you should not blame yourself.

She looked at him for a long time. A tiny tic formed beneath her right eye. He saw the tremor in her hands ruffling the cigarette smoke. Then she invited him over.

For more than a decade, he had fantasized about an occurrence like this. In the fantasies, he was the perfect lover. Afterward, they would both be silent, satisfied, spent. The woman was mostly silent, too. Just a few words as she got up from the bed, the sheet wrapped around her. “Don’t worry. It happens.” She paused on her way to the bathroom and added, “Age is a merciless mistress.”

But I am not even fifty, he thought as he hurriedly dressed and fled.

Over the following weeks, Mr Diggity pestered him for the article. One morning the publisher accused him of backpedalling because he held no sympathy for the deceased. “Little losers. Isn’t that what you called them? Soulless orphans? Hollow shells?” Mr Wardle couldn’t recall if he had used these terms, but it seemed likely.

Eventually, he called the woman. “Hello. It’s me.” There was a long pause, and he realized she couldn’t recognize his voice. Perhaps she had filed him away under “disappointment” or “malfunction” or something. “The journalist. We met . . . ”

“Oh. Did you call earlier? I am sorry if I missed you. I have been so busy.” There was a drag at the centre of all her words, as if she was scolding a spoiled child.

“I actually called about the article.”

There was a brief pause before she said, “We never had time to finish.”

“The article?”

“Yes. What do you think I’m talking about?” When he said nothing, she added with a barely perceptible exhalation, “Can I call you later?” He waited half the night for the call, and the following morning he dialled her number and apologized, muttering something about the editor harassing him for the article. “Did I mention Capricorn was always interested in jewellery? I dreamt of her a couple of nights ago. She wanted to borrow my earrings. Said it was for a special occasion. What do you make of it?"

"I think it's your grief speaking."

"I don't know why people say things like that. Grief speaking." She sounded disappointed and a bit annoyed. "Who knows what happens to the spirit?" She rambled on about a YouTube video that presented consciousness as a transferrable entity. Over the following weeks, she mentioned other signs she had received, and he had to steer her back to her daughter's suicide. Shortly after, Mr Diggity asked about the article and Mr Wardle mentioned that the woman seemed to be getting over her daughter's death.

"Dang, dog. We need grief. Anger. Passion. She might be healing. Move quickly."

But it was too late; the woman had made herself unreachable. She stopped replying to his emails and voice messages. In the parlance of the juveniles, she was ghosting him. He too tried to move on. He wrote articles about sleepy-eyed people who filmed themselves solemnly unboxing products, and spewing advice for hair loss—some of the remedies he tried himself and smelled thereafter like castor oil and sardine for days—and once he wrote about a gangly young man who had shrunk his living space to a closet-size room. But his heart was not in it.

The comments too dried up. Mr Diggity complained about the decreased traffic to his site and asked if there was a problem. Mr Wardle couldn't tell him of his growing obsession with the private life of the suicide's mother. She began an Instagram account using the name Glamourgoat and photographed herself posing at the Humber Bay Bridge and the Gooderham building in Toronto and at the Scarborough Bluffs and Rouge Beach Park. These photographs were always accompanied with trivia of the sort Mr Wardle would have once scorned. "Wrong boots for this place" and "Gosh, look at my hair." At the Port Credit GO station, she was photographed pouting before a crowd of harassed-looking commuters; she wrote the caption, "Bad vibes bring me down." She added filters to some photos, and in others she inserted herself into historic sites. Soon she began to include before and after photos; in some, her daughter was in the before column and in others, the after. She described everyday occurrences as "epic moments." Most of her posts were juvenile, and Mr Wardle couldn't decide whether this was because of her audience or her personality.

She posted each night and the traffic to her site increased, until it was over ten thousand. Who were these viewers? Mr Wardle wondered, and his insomnia returned. Late one night he walked out of his building. Godbolt appeared to be sleeping, but as Mr Wardle passed him, the homeless man said, "I will tell you a secret. I never sleep. Ask me why."

"I don't care, but why?"

"It's because each time I sleep, I forget something about myself. In the mornings I feel the empty space bouncing around my head."

"And?"

Godbolt looked away from him, towards a row of high-rises a block away. "You have asked your question, and I have answered. What the fuck else do you need from me?"

"There's a woman . . . "

"Go on."

"I believe she is channelling her daughter."

"Spirit. It's the only thing that survives." He pointed to a colourful billboard in the distance advertising cellphones. "I see them all the time. Couldn't have survived otherwise. They used to be bleached but they are getting more colourful by the day." He laughed and sank into his shawl. That week, Mr Wardle wrote an article about homelessness and Mr Diggity replied with "WTF," but he published it nevertheless. Mr Wardle knew he was losing his mooring when he began to write about poverty and discrimination and greenhouse gas, topics in which he had no interest.

While *his* world was sinking, Glamourgoat's was thriving. In one of her Instagram posts, she explained that she was starting an online business on Etsy. He followed the link and saw, under the banner "Glamourgoat's Gifts," photographs of necklaces and beads and bangles and one, taken a while ago, of her daughter gazing at a misty lake. On impulse, he created a new email address with a fake name and ordered an item that looked like a fly smasher. Less than an hour later, he got an email asking for a rating. The next night, after a foray into *Wenches on Benches*, he gave her five stars. For our abbreviated act, he thought.

She was effusive in her following emails and sent a list of items she decided he would like. Soon his table was filled with beads, crystals, pendants, and necklaces. All these things he bought because of the hot flush of pleasure her responses evoked ("I am sending a warm piece of me with this pendant" and "This necklace comes from deep inside me.") With each purchase, he cursed himself and decided he would buy nothing more. Yet he stayed up late browsing her various online accounts. He pored over every silly pronouncement. Her post about her daughter's death evoked hundreds of responses, yet a few nights later she wrote, "No two people can travel the same path." Some nights he felt she was simply aping the tactics of the popular influencers, while at other times he felt that this woman who had lost a child simply desired some affirmation.

He missed the uncomplicated pleasures of his previous online forays. The women displaying their breasts and panties had demanded nothing more of him than fifteen minutes or so of his attention. One night he walked out of his building to clear his head. As he approached Godbolt, he noticed the other man rousing himself. "Misery forces us into choices. Is a locked door a hindrance or an opportunity?" He chuckled and added, "The spirits are gathering. Time to hide." He pulled his shawl over his head.

Mr Wardle continued walking but stopped suddenly. He retraced his steps to his apartment and returned with everything he had bought from Glamourgoat. "A gift," he told Godbolt.

Godbolt shrugged off his shawl and dipped into the bag. "Nothing changes, eh? Beads and baubles." He placed the jewellery on the ground carefully, as if he were doing a jigsaw puzzle. Mr Wardle had never seen the homeless man without his expression of surly disinterest, but as he arranged the pieces, his face was stricken with such a violent sadness that Mr Wardle felt he would either rise and strike him or he would weep. Godbolt did neither; instead, he turned away and looked up at the lights on the high-rises. "There are your spirits. You created them, but I can see them." He scattered the jewellery so suddenly Mr Wardle stepped back.

"Remember the woman I told you about? I want to break her hold but I don't know how."

"I have nothing to offer you. Look at me. Do I look like someone with answers?"

His eyes, reflecting the lights from the billboards, seemed to be glowing and Mr Wardle suddenly imagined him as a monk or a shaman watching the world crumble around him. "You are the only one unplugged. You must see things."

Godbolt drew his shawl around him and in a muffled voice said, "I am not a person. I am a condition." He covered himself once more, the shawl rippling like a tattered sail floating in the ocean. Mr Wardle couldn't tell if the sounds from within the man were from tears or laughter. He stood there for a few minutes before he walked away.

Mr Wardle resolved to leave Glamourgoat alone too, ignoring

all her email suggestions. He continued to browse her Instagram and TikTok accounts though, and nine months following his initial interview, she wrote that this would most likely be her last post because she was "moving to Australia for solitude and if it's on the cards, love." Beneath there was a row of Avatar emojis and the confusing sentences, "The dead are never truly dead. They leave only with our permission."

Mr Wardle went to his window, expecting to see the glow of a cigarette beneath. In the morning he was awakened by an ambulance siren, and when he went down, he saw the vehicle departing and a portly man with a waistcoat and bushy sideburns watching the empty spot. "What happened?" Mr Wardle asked him.

The man threw his cigarette away. "Nothing," he said and walked away. Mr Wardle felt a sudden rage and a meandering puckered sadness like a corrosive odour. In that mood, he got out the manuscript he had hidden for so long, scratched out the title and his name, and began rewriting. Each night, as he wrote, he gazed at the empty spot which Godbolt had occupied. Sometimes he felt as if he was in a conversation with the homeless man and so his style and mood shifted. A year later, the slim novel, titled *Neo-Avatars*, was published under the pseudonym Mr Herbert Bumphrey Wardle by a small press. And he excerpted his first chapter to finally finish the article Mr Diggity had long requested.

The departed never really disappear. They hang around as imagined spirits, constantly reanimated by what they have left behind, their lives extended by our grief and desperation. In recreating the dead, we also recreate ourselves . . .

The Morrocoy

The man in the grey overcoat at the end of the crowded bus, reflecting on his doctor's preliminary diagnosis made earlier in the day, almost missed the medical lab. He had never been in this part of the city and he noticed that the embarking passengers' ethnicities seemed to shift with each stop. The more neglected the stop looked, the darker the passengers who got on from there. He pulled the cord at the last moment and the bus stopped with a jerk. He fiddled with the side door while holding his requisition form for the lab.

"Use the front."

He didn't hear at first and the driver repeated his instructions sounding annoyed. The man intended to apologize but as he approached the front exit, as directed, he heard the driver mumbling something about "these people" and "can't understand English."

"I understand English perfectly well, sir."

He hoped his tone was polite because he did not want to get into an argument, but the other man's manner as he stared him up and down, the contempt he packed in his small hard eyes, the way he gestured angrily to the door, gave the man in the overcoat pause, so he added, "I also understand this is not 1970 when it was okay to shout at people like me."

That was the year he arrived from Trinidad, when a brown man on a bus was not as common and a simple night-time stroll would draw the attention of cops. He had been unprepared for these interactions but stood his ground because he was young and brash and not used to the idea that he should feel any different from the men he passed on the streets. Once he was busted up from a scuffle with a pair of hooligans, but while he was running along the dark street from an approaching siren he felt as invigorated as he had been during his teenage boxing bouts when, too, his handsome face was a mess. He never cared.

"Are you going to get off my bus?"

"Your bus?" the man in the overcoat asked softly, again wanting to avoid a confrontation as he slowly made his way to the exit. Before he got there, the bus pulled off so abruptly, he was slammed against a post. He was momentarily confused and he glanced at the other passengers, mostly brown like him, who looked away, not wanting to be involved. But one, a short, chubby fiftyish white man with a stylish beige scarf and a newsboy cap, shrugged supportively at the driver as he exited at the next stop, at a comic book store.

A year and a half after his arrival in the country he had applied for a job as a library assistant in Ajax, a small town east of the city. The town was then populated by people who had fled the bigger cities and by local couples who lived in the old Strawberry Box houses built by their grandparents. Sometimes, while he was shelving books, someone would come up to him and ask, very slowly, as if he could not understand English, about some book or the other. But soon the regulars got used to him, both in the library and the Ananias Café, a small Greek place that sold a strong coffee that reminded him of the parched beans back home.

He was the only brown man in the town, so he was viewed then as an oddity rather than a harbinger.

The decades passed and soon he began to notice the occasional dark face in the library. During those years he, too, changed; he lost the island's loose amiability, its brashness. Perhaps it was his increasing age or the slow pace of the little town with its lacquered politeness, but he preferred to think it was his working with books. If any of his old island friends, familiar with his former recklessness, his skylarking, had spotted him, they would have been astonished at his mellowing. He thought of this sometimes because his reserve gave him the space for self-reflection and an understanding of his place in his new country.

For instance, at one time he would be confused when the newer ethnicities, mostly brown like himself, returned neither his friendliness nor his curiosity; but he soon realized that these people who resembled each other had brought their mutual animosities along with them, which made them suspicious of each other. They were finding their ways. Some would never fit in, but others would, like him, change so gradually they would overlook the hardening skin. It was not personal, so he was never offended. In his view, insecurity made them testy and standoffish; they were looking for alliances that would, in their minds, confirm their acceptance in their new country, not drag them back to their past. He had long since realized that newcomers were troubled by three concerns: work, housing, and where in the social hierarchy they would be assigned.

At the next stop, at Danforth, most of the brown passengers got off. He thought about exiting and finding his way to the lab but decided to stay in the bus until it arrived at the terminal. Once there, he would decide whether he should cancel, or arrive late for his appointment. He gazed at the row of businesses, small structures of identical sizes with Bangladeshi names. He noticed the driver glancing at him in his mirror, and he wondered if perhaps he had had an altercation with someone from that part of the world. He knew that a single hostile encounter could poison the victim's approach to the broader group. The way he sat upright in his seat suggested an alertness to aggression and he recalled reading of drivers who had been spat upon.

The man in the overcoat was brought back to the reason for his trip on the bus. The previous year he had undergone a series of tests to determine the reason for his dyspnea and extreme fatigue. The small-town family doctor he still visited—finding another in the city was impossible—insisted at first that his symptoms were not uncommon among patients approaching seventy and later switched to the supposition that losing his partner had instigated his new debilities.

She was six years older than him and he had first seen her in the library where he worked and where she volunteered on weekends. She was an avid reader and when they met later in the café, she always carried a book. Her apartment, too, was lined with bookcases and he joked once that her interest in him was to sort and classify her books. Because her apartment was bigger than his, he moved in and shared the rent. She was slim, tall and bespectacled, and her face sometimes held a solemn smile as if she were bundling a scatter of memories. They were friends rather than lovers, both comfortably attuned to solitude—he from the years of living in Canada, she from the early death of her husband—and it was three months before they finally slept together. That was eighteen years ago and he was fifty at the time.

When he looked back at that period, he felt he was comfortable rather than happy, the latter condition seeming too expansive, with sparks of spontaneous fervour and an assured extroversion, which he had lost. Still he always believed they would grow old together. Her cancer was sudden and aggressive and in half a year she was gone. Months later, he arranged and rearranged her books and tidied the place up as if she was on a trip abroad and would soon return. Eventually he packed everything in boxes and took them to the library and a Sally Ann centre. He realized that he was trying to remove all traces of her from the apartment, but during the nights he unconsciously dimmed the lights to her preferred setting, slept on his side of the bed, awoke early to make the cinnamon tea she liked. In the café he now sat alone and grew quietly disturbed whenever anyone came across to his table.

"Are you new?" He glanced across, puzzled by the Black woman who had come to sit next to him, having moved from the back. She was stout under her coat and appeared middle-aged though she could have been much older. "I don't mean to pry but I noticed . . . " She hesitated as if unsure about his reaction.

"Yes?"

"I noticed your confusion. You have to get used to this or your life will be hell. Forget about what you did back home." The bus stopped at a traffic light and a trio of teenage girls hopped on.

When he realized what she meant he told her, "Back home was a long time ago. But I am new to Toronto." He was still slightly dazed from the recent blow to his head. "Not exactly new. I lived here for a couple months. Thirty years ago." He saw the curiosity in her eyes and added, "I moved to a small town for a job. My wife . . . we were not married but I think of her that way. She died suddenly."

"Sorry to hear that. What made you return here? Too many memories back there?"

He shook his head. "She was the only real friend there. The others were . . . they were acquaintances."

She seemed to be reflecting on his response. "I planning to leave at the end of the year," she said finally. "Me no want me grave to harden with ice." He understood her shift to an island accent was to give more resonance to her confession, but he was touched by the intimacy of the twang. "Besides, me can't put up with all of this anymore. Like what just happen to you. It add up after all the years and unless you skin hard like morrocoy, it bound to hurt. But people is not morrocoy. People is people. And that bump on you forehead going to get worse in a few hours. Rub something on it. Canadian Healing Oil, if you could find it." She chuckled and added, "Funny, eh?"

"What is?"

"Nothing. Sometimes you got to laugh at everything otherwise you will go crazy." She got up. "Alright, you take care. My stop coming up." She pulled the cord and walked with deliberate slowness to the front, as if daring the driver to pull off.

He put his hand to his forehead and tried to trace the bump. He glanced at his watch. The bus was now passing through an incline of small cottage-style houses and the remaining passengers, comfortably dressed, were either sleeping or reading, as if preparing for a long trip. The road here was not as congested and he remembered his first trip to Ajax, the grazing cattle on stretches of farmland, and the occasional bungalow that came as a surprise. He was captivated. He himself had come from a little village and he had always been drawn to pastoral descriptions of uncluttered areas where the pace was leisurely and predictable.

Life there was certainly different from the city. There was no outright hostility and although his greetings were never acknowledged, he sometimes caught a lingering glance he could never interpret. In time though he became a fixture in the library, a sight as familiar as the creaky window overlooking the wooded area or a shelving cart. *Then* the withheld questions were asked: Where was he from? No, *really* from? Was he not happy to escape the war or famine or whatever had propelled him to leave? Once an old woman at the post office posed this question and in his usual manner, he gave a brief generic response about being a single child of parents who had passed away early. “There’s nothing to be ashamed of, you know,” she said sceptically. “We all come from a place of hardship.” She described the life of a woman who was perpetually thankful to be free of all the restrictions and the poverty she had always known. As he recalled her description of this grateful immigrant, he wondered how the Black woman who had just left would have reacted if he’d mentioned to her he worked in a library there too and his life was relatively comfortable. Once he actually went that route in the café and the elderly man listening sceptically seemed disappointed as if he had sanitized his life.

The bus was now in the Kennedy area and he gazed out at the factories and warehouses. Steam rose from the chimneys and vents. He glanced at the new passengers boarding at this stop, the different colours, and he wondered how many of them would have given the woman in the post office a more amenable story; a tale of brutality and silence and finally escape. The older passengers, those around his age, still in their factory overalls, appeared too exhausted to exhume their hardships for anyone, and the group of teenagers chatting at the back, their accents wholly of this country, were likely unburdened by distant narratives of shame. They must have heard snatches of their parents’ stories about all they had relinquished to get here and the additional sacrifices just to survive. Scrimping on food, worried about rent, making enough to barely survive. The children would have listened to versions of “We doing all of this for your sake,” so many times, it no longer scratched.

At the Ananias Café, the men and women who gathered there daily, older than him by a decade or more, often spoke in generalities, their prejudices never fully drawn out and softened by their folksy descriptions. He found himself focusing on the loopy humour rather than the cavalcade of regrets. In time, he realized this anger at their diminishing status was central to all their concerns about foreign language signs and the economy and diversity hiring and congestion.

As he recalled these conversations, he wondered why he had not offered his own opinions more forcefully at the time instead of being amused by their eccentricities. In the beginning, he had been astonished at their candidness in his presence but soon he began to write off their views as the crackpot eccentricities of old men who had a decade left to live at the most, who held no real social power and whose opinions had become calcified from fraying memories. They were harmless, he convinced himself, and just like back home, they likely evoked embarrassment from their grandchildren. Their time had passed. Now he wondered if his silence had given them permission, or worse, served as a tacit agreement.

The Black woman's simple, almost childlike allusion affected him because he suspected that hidden within its sympathetic covering was a hint of accusation. In this uneasy mood, he began to think of all the new immigrants who walked past him to the other librarians as if they were afraid he would speak their language or open a box they had shut tightly. They were constantly nervous as if their inventions might be found out. One afternoon he heard a brown woman describing to a librarian all the comforts, the servants and bungalows she had left behind. He felt embarrassed for her, not because she was boasting but because her tone was one of pleading.

The bus stopped and a young man with a hoodie got on. He was dressed in baggy jeans and a puffy coat and he flopped, legs wide apart, on a seat in the middle of the vehicle as if he owned it. The driver followed his move on his rear-view mirror. The man in the overcoat remembered when he, too, was brimming with youthful confidence; when he'd shrug off those who rankled him because he believed that, in most groups, he was the smartest, the nimblest, the funniest, and so on.

The bus swung into the Scarborough station and he walked to the exit. He wanted the driver, who was pushing a thermos into a pouch, to look up and give him an opportunity to say something. But what? An insult? He had seen how outrage often reduced brown men like him into funny, farcical creatures. He walked into the terminal and at the highway he hesitated and turned. Through the glass door he saw the driver dismounting. He watched the man's unsteady gait, the way he favoured one leg, the good foot struggling to carry the bulk. On the bus, seated, he had appeared taller and more threatening.

At the turnstile, a young man, just behind him, asked impatiently, "You going through or not?" The young man's accent blunted the statement so he could not be sure if it was demand or enquiry.

He stepped aside and as a group of harassed-looking men gibbering on their cellphones pushed past him, he shouted, "Sorry. I am a morrocoy. This is my pace."

He had no idea why he attempted a joke no one would understand but then he heard a chuckle, each note loud and clear. "Yes, yes," he heard, "Exactly. That is the tune. Disappearing in slow motion." The crackling laugh grew louder and seemed to enclose the clanking of an approaching train, startling a flock of pigeons that surrounded the homeless man, who each morning fed them crumbs of bread as he sang in an impossible falsetto, " . . . walking on a one-way street . . . any way, any way, any way, no-ooh."

My Better Half

Whether death taps me on the shoulder or punches me to the ground will make no difference. I am eighty-two years old and this body belongs to a different time. Do not think I am bitter, it has served me well. Every wrinkle hides a story and some stories cannot be repeated in polite company, as I told Arlene, the saucy nurse who comes to my house once a week. She laughs easily, this girl, and when I joked that if I were thirty years younger and all my bits still working, I would have found another use for the massage table she brings along for my physiotherapy, she made it a point to roll her end when she walked away. Good strong stock with thick calves beneath a body designed for a farm. She never talks much about her life, which suits me just fine, because I am not interested in idle blather about brats or struggling to make ends meet or whatever madness young people nowadays talk about.

I began to miss the old days even more after my Nancy passed away. The little town where everyone knew each other and the jokes we heard as kids still seemed fresh a generation later. Some of these jokes would be considered salty and offensive now but we had no care for people who find a way to put daggers into everything. Some of them have made their way into my town and they stride along the streets as if they have built our houses, fought our wars, tilled our land, understand who we are. I'm all for anyone who puts his mind to a fair day's wage, and who values the pleasure of seeing the task complete, and nothing knocks the wind out of me more than to see all these slackers mooching outside the stores and gibbering to each other.

There's no greater pleasure to be had in simple things like watching a calf make its first stumbling steps, or leaping into a pond, or harvesting berries, though I guess none of this will appeal to folks who hanker for shiny doohickeys as soon as these are cooked up. When I was a lad, me and all my chums would spend an hour with the cows before we trooped off to school half a mile away and twice that time when we got home. Winters were not the pussycat affairs we have nowadays, so we kept our eyes out for each other and if someone had a terrible year, we all chipped in without a second's thought. The farm buildings were set up for farrow to finish hogs, and during the town fairs or square dances in the community centre, it was still possible to get a whiff of the hog perfume above that of Arbege and Old Spice.

Most of the farms are gone now and Main Street—where I saw my favourite barber who remembered the exact dates of our last visits, and across the road the butcher who knew the type of cuts we wanted before we crossed his door, and the baker who looked like Li'l Abner from the comic strip but who was born for the job—is now congested with outsiders who swarm back to their high-rises and shelters, subsidized by people who have either beetled off, are stored in a nursing home, or, like me, trapped in a place that seems more unfamiliar by the day. Not that I ever go out much, but I remember the time when I would walk from one end of Main Street to the other and recognize every single person my eyes caught. Even with those who were unfamiliar, I would, in five minutes or less, discover an uncle or cousin I knew. It's not only the relatives, because we were also familiar with each other's language, antics, supper, prayers, dreams, ambitions, and everything else.

Now everyone's a stranger and I am not talking only of the outsiders in their costumes but also of the young ones who walk around with appliances plugged into their ears and wouldn't know a feed grinder or double-bottom plough if it hit them squarely in the arse. Too much time on their hands, if you ask me, which is why they sulk and protest as if the bloody world is coming to an end and only they can fix it. The men and women who built this place are, in their eyes, relics of an unwelcome time.

If I close my eyes, I can still see the girls in crinoline dresses and puffy skirts and the boys with their cigarettes rolled up into their sleeves, sneaking little glances or tipping their caps as they passed each other on the streets. Young ones today look down on that time but everyone was respectful and knew their place. The cops were nicer too and the worst they would do was give us a dressing down and threaten to talk to our parents. It was one big family where all the guests were properly invited. There were correct seating arrangements and everyone knew their place. No skipping the line or jumping to the front. *This* is the picture I want in my head when I kick the bucket.

Arlene sometimes talks of some of her other patients, who have forgotten so much they are like toddlers learning to walk, and even though I know this is not by choice, I sometimes wonder if it's not a kind of cruel blessing, if there is such a thing, to be stuck in a time when the world was young and we were all heroes. I mentioned this to Arlene and she said, "You've got the most important thing still working," and before I could disagree with a naughty joke, she added, "Your heart. You wouldn't want to be in that state. Trust me." She's right, I know, even if she pays extra attention when I stray down that lane and tell her about my courtship of Nancy and the life we lived before she passed on.

That was seven years, three months and eleven days ago and when, after a spell of falls, the last one serious enough to rejig my thinking that I could maintain my own upkeep, I went to the retirement home she'd been in and requested the room where stayed her last four months. I remained there for two weeks, regretting my decision every day. I discovered I did not want to die in a strange place hooked up with tubes overseen by swarthy strangers. I guess in this way I am different from Nancy, who was always comfortable in new situations. She was okay almost till the end, thank God, and on the days I visited thrice a week, she got her nurses to attend to her appearance and to make sure her hair was combed and her clothes extra spiffy. In the last week of her life, her breathing began to fail but even when she was hooked up to her ventilator and could no longer eat solid food, she had a smile on her face. I'd been in all sorts of scraps in my life, fought off diseases, almost drowned in a creek when I was twelve, watched a cousin lose his leg in a boiler accident and another donate two fingers to a threshing machine; I delivered calves and watched others die before they hit the ground but this I could not take.

I never showed my Nancy how I felt but I am sure she knew. On the evening before her eyes closed forever, she squeezed my hand a little and may the Lord strike me down if I am lying but I swear I saw, for a minute, the girl I'd first glimpsed in our church, all angel-like with her white gloves and her curly red hair pressed into a bonnet.

She was not all angel, I discovered early on, but she mostly kept my paws off her throughout high school and at the sock hops and community dances and even in the Chevy I bought just before we got hitched. She may have weakened, but she knew her own mind. Everything that was worthwhile, I learned from her.

Soon after Arlene began her sessions with me, I told her of our courtship, and she said, "Poor woman. How did she put up with all of this?" This is how Arlene speaks sometimes, suddenly showing a serious face, so I can't say if her joking has ended. She seems about thirty-five and she once mentioned she'd been around the blocks a few times, but in my books, she is still a little sprig. Maybe because we never had children of our own, Nancy and I, it's difficult to understand young folks. There was no need, really. We had each other and whenever there was a point of confusion, one or the other would chip in with an explanation. Nancy was more refined than I was with folks up to no good, and she didn't like it when I said that she constantly wanted to harvest crops from barren land. We had our differences like most couples married for fifty-three years but these arguments never got out of hand and when we were finished stating our views, we were gracious with each other. Sometimes I would tell her that these sermons sounded great in church but had no practical value in the real world and she would sigh and call me a "barmy old coot," followed by "But you're my old coot."

For sure our lives would have been different if we had had a family. I would not have sold off the farm the year I hit sixty and Nancy would not have wasted her time with all these charitable groups and food banks and organizations bothering about refugees and single mothers and the like. I have nothing against anyone who has been softened up by some hardship and who might be in genuine need of help, but I do not agree with constantly paying for the delinquencies of repeat offenders who know there will always be a cushion. At a different time, we all had to pick ourselves up with no assistance and we were stronger for it. We knew there would be rainy days ahead and we squirreled away whatever we could.

Now we have people from all over the world streaming into our cities and the people in power seem more interested in the welfare of these strangers than those of us who built this place from the ground up. It's going to get worse according to the dailies Arlene brings along each Wednesday. The gangs and the shootings are seeping out from Toronto and creeping closer to our town every week. In my day, if we had a gripe, we fought it out hand to hand like real men, not firing from cars and speeding away. The world is spinning at a different pace now. Everyone wants something for free and the fastest way they can get whatever they want is by whining about how difficult things are for them. It seems to work too, this harping on privilege and discrimination. Maybe it's taught now in schools, all these shiny new catchphrases. I'd wager that if you ask a schoolchild anything of the Hudson Bay Company or the War of 1812, you would likely get a blank stare.

I worry about my country and sometimes I think that this is the right time to make my exit. A couple weeks earlier, I was reading the papers and I came across an article about students who wanted to be excluded from some class that offended their culture or some such nonsense. "This is why this country is going downhill," I told her. "Instead of bringing people together we are dragging them apart. There's a race to see who can be the most put-upon." She had none of her usual cheeky reply for me that day, but during her next visit, I pointed to a photograph of a half-breed family and told her, "Blended, they say. Just like the ingredients you throw into a mixer or what comes out of a thresher. In my day—"

"In your day, they would have been strung up and horse-whipped."

She seemed so angry, I told her, "Whoa there, girl. I'm talking about all these new fancy words for everything. Blended. Makes it seem all nice and easy. That's all I meant."

"I know what you meant," she said quietly, and for the rest of the session, she remained quiet.

When she was packing up, I told her, "I didn't mean to offend you, dear. You shouldn't take it so personal."

"I try not to," she said and her lips barely moved when she spoke.

Now what could she mean by that? I wondered after she'd left and the question remained with me until her next session. So all the while she was stretching and coaxing my old bones, I was looking at her in a new way to see if there was something I missed. Maybe there was an Indian in her family tree way back but even so, she looked no different from any of the girls at the school I attended. If that was the case, though, I should put her mind at ease by telling her I have nothing against Indians who have been pushed aside because they are not as good with all this new-age blarney as everyone else. If anyone should make a fuss about anything, it should be them because they didn't suddenly arrive with their suitcases filled with demands long after everything was built from the ground up. I didn't get a chance to tell Arlene any of this because midway in her session she asked me, "Was Nancy your only woman?"

"Just you and her," I said and she chuckled in a way that made me forget her earlier restlessness.

"Was she very pretty?"

"She was special. Not in the way they use the word nowadays but special in the way her eyes lit up with stars when she was pleased and with fire when she was riled."

"Was she riled often?"

I was about to say, What woman isn't, but caught myself in time to say instead, "Sometimes, but a stranger wouldn't know because she wore her smile well. She was pretty as hell, to answer your first question. Looked like Elaine Stewart, the actress who was in all these Westerns."

"Did you ever tell her this? That she was pretty?"

"Every morning. Every blessed morning. Rain, sun, or sleet,

it was how I greeted her." I thought Arlene would be pleased with this but her fingers on my back seemed to crumble and I thought once more that I knew nothing of this girl who came into my home every week. "What about you, my dear?" I asked her. "Anyone special in your life?"

"Roll over," she said. "We need to get to your shoulders."

This was the pattern for the next couple of weeks. Arlene would ask about Nancy but whenever I doubled-back her curiosity, she avoided my questions. She had some trouble in her life for sure. Maybe a lousy husband or a messy divorce. She never liked it when I began my sentences with "In my day . . . " so I never mentioned that at a different time, her man would have seen her through to the end. But her questions about Nancy also brought back a little spark in my life, as these rusty old memories reminded me of how lucky I'd been. For such a long time too.

I also hoped that Arlene would begin to see a better side than the one she had latched on to. I sometimes believed her interest in my early life was because there were no equivalent memories in her own messed up childhood. I liked these questions because it was good to talk about something other than medical matters. Once, she asked me, "Have you ever thought of how a son, if you had one, would have turned out?"

Many, many times, I told her, "Would've been like me. Stubborn as a mule but with a heart of gold."

She rolled her eyes and asked, "And a daughter?"

"Oh, I'm sure you already know the answer. A sparkling beauty, with her mother's eyes and her half-smile. Like another Elaine Stewart, although I don't know if this look still holds. Standards have changed for the worse." Because she said nothing, I asked her, "And what about you, my dear? Any little ones?"

"A boy. And he looks nothing like me," she added quickly. "Now roll over."

"You should bring him along sometime. There's a big backyard for him to do his mischief."

"He's at school," she said in a tone that told me she did not want any further discussion.

"Understood."

After a while, she said, "I'm going to take him out. Move him to Brampton."

That was all she said and after she'd left, I wondered why she would move him to a town filled with problems. Gangs and overcrowding and people who barely spoke English. The poor lad would be like a fish out of water. I didn't tell her that her son wouldn't be the only one discommoded by her move, because it would sound selfish on my part. But she must have sensed this concern because during the following session she told me I needn't worry too much because she'd contacted a physiotherapist with excellent credentials. While she was digging into her purse for a card, I told her point-blank, "I know you don't like me to talk about how much the place has changed and crime and gangs and all that but you must understand I have only your best interest when I say that you have to think carefully before you make this decision. Things are getting tricky here too but it's not as bad as Brampton. The schools are a mess according to the dailies. The poor lad will hardly understand the folks there."

She listened carefully before she said, "He will be fine."

"I am going to be blunt, my dear. Here, he will be around his own kind."

The stroke of her fingers changed and I could tell she was mad as hell and although she said nothing for a long while, I knew at that moment why she had been so annoyed with my talk of the old days and why she refused my invitation to bring along her son to explore the backyard. She was kneading so deeply into my back I began to flinch and once a soft sound escaped my mouth.

She stopped briefly then and her strokes grew gentler until I could barely feel her manipulation. As at so many times during her sessions, I felt drowsy. "You are loosening up," she told me in the rustling flack parents use with toddlers.

"That's good," I said in what I hoped was a light voice. "Parts of me are seizing up like an old tractor."

There was a pause as if she was considering my statement. "Tell me about Nancy," she asked eventually.

"What do you want to hear?"

"Anything you choose to say."

I realized this would be our last conversation so I told her once more of my first sight of Nancy at church and pursuing her at school and finally giving her my class ring and our few visits to Toronto, she in her Oxford loafers, for the concerts she enjoyed and my pain during her final hours and how I would have done anything to transfer her suffering to me so that she would be just Nancy again, the woman with the sparkling eyes and the little smile. She was half of me, I said. My better half.

Loki

They have mostly disappeared, people my age. They pop up in the new dangerous world of dreadful lockdowns like gophers to get food and drugs. I cannot blame them. We are at the age where any exposure could be fatal. We see these dire warnings each evening on the news. Two years ago, there were reports of the elderly in multigenerational homes struck down by their asymptomatic grandchildren, and I was glad I lived alone.

I used to find much enjoyment in life. Or rather, in living. I hosted parties for the free-spirited and the newly free. It was an odd but lively group. Immigrants. Draft dodgers. Cricketers. Musicians. Rebels. We were hoisted towards the nights on drunken, lively arguments. We celebrated the closing of the seventies, that miserable decade of shortages and wars. There were new worries about creeping corporate influences. About Reagan and Thatcher. But it was a buoyant time for the young and youngish. The world seemed to be shifting to simpler times. Neon clothes. Mixed tapes. Pink Floyd. Hip-hop. Blockbuster.

My guests departed early the next morning. In time, one visitor lingered. Longer each visit. We planted gooseberries and a pear tree which bore its first fruit in five years. I harvested these fruits with another visitor. Her view of the world was too stringent for one so attractive. That's what I thought when I saw her each evening beneath the pear tree with her notebook. We went to poetry readings at the Art Bar and lectures at Massey Hall. Nights in Algonquin. Weekends in Banff. Carnivals in Trinidad. At the Toronto Western Hospital, she remembered the tree. Held my hand and said I should let it grow.

I mentioned this wish to the purchaser one year later. There were fewer visitors to my new place, the music softer, arguments withheld. Still, the world seemed repairable. I travelled alone then. To Bali. Thailand. Burma. That part of the world. Travellers look for elaborations. Clarifying tapestries. I looked only for simplicity. A little village. A rustic temple. A kneeling monk. My world, to the end. That was what I imagined.

It's strange we never prepare for the only predictable event in our life. Maybe it's a form of superstition. Planning for something will hasten its occurrence. Better to kick it down the road. Until I turned seventy-three, two years ago, I treasured my solitude. No obligations. No compromises and subtle hypocrisies. My route had shortened, but I could still choose the destination. A pub here, a coffee shop there. A quiet walk in the park or the waterfront trail. I imagined an unremarkable fadeout.

I now believe our perspectives are ordered by the degrees of choice we possess. A sanctuary narrows into a prison. A pleasurable activity hardens into a ritual. A ritual changes into an obsession. And so on. I know it would be wise to avoid these speculations. They add no wisdom, nothing but a stabilizing fatalism. They remind me of Napoleon the Third in Zola's, *La Debacle*, indifferently striding forward to meet his fate, while "bullets fell in concert with a music like the fierce autumnal blasts."

Some of my old acquaintances are in long-term care. They, too, must feel like Zola's Napoleon. Their children complain about loss of contact during this pandemic. Forced to wave from windows. Watching the steady stream of deaths. They lament the disappearing of the aged. I do not know if their anger is not mixed with guilt. I cannot understand this relationship. I do not know either if those who are stacked away in nursing homes dream they are elsewhere. If they imagine the smell of children's socks and morning coffee and a wet dog somewhere. Or if the firm hands holding the spoon and the soap belong to someone they have known over the years.

I should state here that I was recently diagnosed with Parkinson's. I tried to view this as the beginning of a story. Once upon a time, a man who was shaving cut himself, so he grew a beard. A month later, a cup fell from his hand and he replaced his chinaware with enamel. Not long after, he slipped on the stairway so he bought himself a cane. He adjusted with each change. When his speech began to slur, he wrote his groceries and other lists on a notepad which he took with him everywhere. But the man could not keep up with the pace of changes. He was constantly tired and once he fainted when he rose from the sofa. He wiped away the blood from his forehead and—

Here, the story stops. I cannot find a moral, a redeeming resolution. There is nothing tidy about disintegration. At the end, most of our choices are made by others. In a crisis, this becomes more noticeable. Television doctors have uttered a word to which I never paid attention. Triaging. The doling out of scarce resources. The predictive ability to survive. It sounds terrible, this word with an ominous geometric ring, yet this cold-eye view of disposability follows every biological law.

The early morning throws up frothy memories. It takes a while to be certain they are not dream residues. Maybe these haphazard wanderings into distant landscapes are valiant last-ditch battles. This morning, I recalled a grove of towering bamboo and darting sabres of light. That forest at the back of our house in Trinidad was my first sanctuary. An escape from the confusion of extended relatives and the constant whine of band saws. I was ten or eleven, and on weekends, accompanied by Bruno, our dog, I took my copies of *Coral Island* or *Robinson Crusoe* and pretended we were alone in the world. I stayed there until I heard my mother's faint voice calling me for some task or the other. Later, as my journeys lengthened, I brought other books with me. These I carried from place to place, packing them neatly in crates and boxes.

I am afraid their journey, like mine, is drawing to a close. I have already begun my divesting. It's an unpleasant task, doing this alone. I have no idea if the browsers at Sally Ann will understand these relationships. A week ago, I felt like crying when I packed into a box my copy of *The Anatomy of Melancholy* by Robert Burton. The woman, now gone, who had gifted me the book had underlined passages she believed I would like. "To walk amongst orchards, gardens, bowers, mounts, and arbours, artificial wildernesses, green thickets, arches, groves . . . between wood and water . . . "

Now during my stuttering walks among sofa, desk, sink, washroom, I must be careful where I place my feet. I know all the spots and cracks in my bedroom. The paint has flaked away on the ceiling. The grout on the windowsill has hardened; in the nights, it resembles bleached bones. The nail indentations near the baseboard heater remind me of chalk outlines from forensic television shows. At the centre of the room, a discoloured patch seems like dried blood. Likely the normal process of weathering. Everything has a due date. I notice these things now.

From my front window, I also notice there are fewer children on the trail leading to the park. Those I spot are different somehow. More observant, it would appear, although this could simply be the yoke of anxiety they carry around. I cannot fully gauge how difficult it must be for children to be barricaded in their homes for so long. If we are shaped by the pivotal events of our generation, how would they turn out in the coming decades? Empaths or psychopaths?

I try to be discreet with my gazing so I don't appear like a solitary crazy. Two days ago, I heard an ambulance siren and saw a stretcher removing a woman who lived with her grandson and half a dozen cats. I soon noticed in every house there were subtle shifts of curtains, blinds tweaked apart, drapes crinkled at the sides. I was not alone, as I imagined. Perhaps in other quiet streets, there are communities of housebound seniors gazing longingly, or fearfully, outside. Many must wonder if this is it, then. Gazing at death, "a bluish decoction in a cup without a saucer." *Death* was the poem's name, I believe. I read it in the coffee shop where, in another world, I would take a book and sit quietly for hours.

Two of my old acquaintances from that coffee shop, now closed, have passed away. I learned of this from a couple whose emails I have blocked. Once the couple was boring and normal, but they have embraced conspiracy theorists raving about vaccines and microchips and government control. Before I blocked the couple, I noticed how much their language had changed, grown more strident.

On the island where I spent my youth there were cricketing metaphors for everything. An old man or woman was constantly "dodging bouncers." The diseased were on "sticky wickets." There is a peculiar comfort in reverting to old vocabularies, even those that nowadays might be considered unsympathetic. So I find myself rereading books I first opened a generation ago. Prior to the pandemic, I had grown frustrated with the newish books I saw in the library. They all seemed to be angling towards a communal chord rather than allowing space for refection. They were not the type of books one would reread. Their value resided only in the initial fever.

Perhaps in stressful times, we wrap ourselves around anything familiar. It's comforting, but there are trade-offs. Foraging around the cobwebs makes the present less real. So, occasionally, I forget small things. Did I shut the front door after I put out the garbage? Did I turn off the stove? I sometimes grow angry when I am searching for my phone, socks, the television remote.

Today a handwritten note in my mailbox informed me of the passing of the neighbour across the road. The note, presumably from the grandson, mentioned that he needed a temporary home for his grandmother's pets. I now have a calico cat that looks at me suspiciously when I pour his food and water into the feeding appliances the grandson provided. The young man had seemed surprised by my offer. As I was, too, when I saw the size of the creature he hauled over in a basket. I was expecting a kitten I could entertain with a ball of twine. "Loki's been round the block," he told me guiltily as if he had made a ruthless calculation. "He's retired now."

Retired was an understatement. The cat never budges from its spot on a coffee table overlooking the window. I don't know if, besieged by memories of better days, he is gazing at his old home. Sometimes, I ask, "What are you seeing?" My voice sounds strange, with hollow pockets, like a radio announcer's obituaries. I pose other questions. How did you get your name? Do cats experience loneliness?

I also apologize whenever I spill some of his food. I tell him of my Parkinson's. How I first assumed the shakiness was temporary and caused by stress or lack of exercise. I talk of my childhood. Moving to this country. The passing of the woman who had also arrived from a distant place. My healing trips following her death and those of my parents. I have asked several times whether he misses his old owner.

I tell him there will be no one to mourn me. To see my

unmarked face in sepia photographs and grainy videotapes. To know that the old song on the radio was among my favourites or the sweater in a thrift store resembled one I favoured. No one to roll their eyes and repeat a joke I made at family dinners. No Facebook reminders of my birthday. I will have disappeared as if I had never been here. I insist this is not the way the world operates. There are always ripples and vestiges. A living thing changes into a dead thing but it does not die.

Loki listens attentively, his head slightly inclined as if he is trying to make sense of my ramblings. I continue this conversation each supper, bemoaning my extinction while still reassuring him, and myself, that there is something I am missing. One night I ask if he will recognize me, if in another life he is reborn as a jungle cat and I a little mammal. He stretches his front paws and gazes up at me as if he is truly intrigued, so I explain my grandparents' belief in transmigration, souls flowing from one body to another.

I cannot be certain he is comfortable, as I am unable to decipher feline dispositions. Most cats in repose appear satisfied. The internet should be helpful, but I get waylaid by videos of cats looking regal, being startled, in ridiculous outfits. And so on. On the bright side, I possess, once more, a routine. I get out of bed earlier. I no longer postpone or skip my meals. I engage in conversations. (Monologues, really.) Some of my curiosity has returned. Selfishness, I think, is not the natural state when you have a dependent.

Most surprising of the changes is the renewed pleasure in preparing my meals. Carefully cutting, steaming, simmering. The kitchen smells of herbs instead of frozen dinners. This has finally drawn Loki from his perch. I tell him I was once like this many years ago. I describe the parties I hosted and the Caribbean dishes I prepared. He looks up at me as if he is trying to gauge my mood.

It's better these days to be truthful.

Many of my conversations are about my journeys. Back in the old country, shuffled from relative to relative. Always curious. Looking at each upheaval as an adventure. The trip to this country, a gamble on a grand scale. Trying to learn something new from each factory and warehouse in which I worked during my first year. I describe the temples in Bali. The monks in Thailand. The unexpected pleasure of meeting a like-minded traveller a thousand miles away. I tell him of my wish, instigated by a book I had read, to visit Patagonia.

The conversations have invaded my daytime naps. Sometimes, I am awakened by the chime of a bell or the tinkling of a singing bowl or the chant of a congregation and it's a while before I recognize my phone's ringtone or the snow removal trucks or a streetcar's rumble. I reveal all of this to Loki. I ask whether he dreams of running around in an orchard and climbing trees. Eyeing the squirrels. He is a predator, after all. Maybe if this lockdown continues for much longer, pets will turn against their owners. I ask him and he bares his teeth. I still cannot understand his moods. But I believe we have grown used to each other's presence. I don't know who will go first and I prefer not to think of this. I will just enjoy this little reprieve. It can be taken away any day.

The Halfway Indian

The enemy of joy is not discontent but disinterest. I remember this proclamation from him soon after I arrived in his country. I say "his country" because of the manner with which he so effortlessly claimed the land and its rituals. He had nothing good to say about Trinidad, the island from which his arrival had preceded mine by close to thirty years. The people there were philistines and marauders who had ransacked a thriving little outpost once they got independence. He made it seem as if they were unfit to govern themselves. They had dismantled the railways, abandoned the botanical gardens, clogged the waterways, replaced seasoned civil servants with hacks. And everywhere, revelry had overtaken progress.

During the first week or so, I assumed his opinionated attitude was characteristic of all established immigrants and was just thankful he had decided to rent me his basement apartment until I found my own place. I wasn't even concerned by his directive that I not interact with him unless I was summoned—which he in fact did every evening during my six weeks in his basement, to accompany him on his one-hour walk. He was a stylishly goateed man of medium built whose coats and hats always appeared a size too big. He might have seemed clownish in his oversized clothes, but his careful, almost military way of walking, leg and cane moving in tandem, striking the ground at the same time, drew second glances. "You see that gentleman there?" he said once, pointing his cane at a homeless man. "He is what we call a native. Look at him. This is what happens when you corral a people accustomed to roaming the land. You put a hold on their dreams. Do you have dreams?" He walked quickly as if he was not interested in my answer.

Mitra was a relative of my father and was the only person from my parents' list who had any time for me. Their other contacts assumed I was intent on sponging off their generosity and they claimed either they were busy with work and their children's activities or occupied with renovations. I was not aware these were excuses at the time, until Mitra enlightened me once when I innocently repeated their apologies. "Whenever these people see a new immigrant, they spot a reflection of themselves they have struggled to scrub away. They are running away not from people like you but from all their little fears, you see."

I was impressed with this observation. I was naïve to the ways of my new country and it was Mitra who outlined what he called the "immigrant narrative of deprivation and endless struggle" that each wave flung against those that followed. His careful manner of speaking, beginning slowly, gaining traction before slowing once more, added a solemn rhythm to his declarations as if he were delivering a scholarly paper. He had retired five years earlier as a government statistician, but his utterances were those of a jaded philosopher. I had met no one like him and was moved to admiration when he said things like, "All changes, bar none, begin with invisible ripples. We never notice until the appearance of the tsunami," or "Everyone is reactive, you see. The only people not reactive are psychopaths," or "We are forever running away from what we assume are inferior versions of ourselves."

He seemed a man of the world, intelligent and filled with wide-ranging ideas. His accent, which combined a British inflection, American bounciness, and, occasionally, an island lilt, made his proclamations appear both intimate and ground-breaking. He subscribed to *The New Yorker* and *Harper's* and the *National Review* and a clutch of international newspapers he stacked on his desk. I concluded that my father's opinion of him was likely motivated by jealousy. My father often recalled Mitra's family's visits during their trips to the island beach, when they would expect their Vauxhall to be loaded with gifts of fruits. "And this little pissing-tail boy dressed up in khaki short pants and socks like a damn tourist, standing by the car with his hands folded as if the mud will stick to him. Always feeling he better than anyone else. A real halfway Indian." My father had fallen into the habit of condemning town-dwellers like Mitra's family as imitative and hypocritical—"follow-fashion" was the term he used. He felt they were like *mapipire* snakes, quick to slip out of their skin.

Because I was certain my father had misjudged him, I was determined not to fall in the same trap. And so I forgave Mitra's little discourtesies as stemming from a mind too grand to be concerned with irrelevant courtesies. After all, he had pointed out the parts of the city where rent was affordable and had given me advice about used-clothing stores and the importance of first impressions and not depending on anyone. To express my gratitude, I did odd jobs around his apartment. I stained his coffee table and chairs, cleaned the grout in his washroom, repainted the hallway quarter-round, repotted his philodendron, sanded his kitchen countertop, and replaced the grommets on his blackout curtains. He would glance up from his stack of newspapers while I was doing all of this, occasionally pouring himself a glass of sherry. Afterwards, instead of expressing appreciation, he told me stories about the furniture I had adjusted. The coffee table he had spotted in a garage sale piled with Nazi paraphernalia; the bookcase held hardcovers signed by famous writers—whom he dismissed as plagiarists—and the sofa had seen a lot of unspecified "action." I felt his accounts far exceeded any expressions of gratitude.

One of his stories involved a Black man who had fallen into difficulties. "It was a year or so after my arrival and I was interested in the escritoire behind which he was seated, overlooking his garage sale. I complimented him on the piece and offered him a ridiculous amount, but he turned it down. He must have seen that I was new to the country and was showing off. He understood me better than I did. I was guilty of the old colonial flaunting, you see. Eventually, he asked me, rather firmly, to leave." Because of the singsong lilt—an island signal of mockery—to his confession, I thought he was criticizing the seller, but he added, "That man taught me an important lesson that day. He taught me that snobbery is just as important as humility." Mitra went on about how a world of only apologetic, modest people would soon sink into mediocrity. Humility is good in movies, he asserted. In real life, it stems from shame.

A couple of days later, during one of our walks, he slowed down to observe a taxi driver stopped by a cop. "Look at that fella wagging his head. Do you know what that head-wag says? It says, 'Please strike me again. I am worthless and deserve it.'"

I felt this was unfair. "It's just a cultural trait. Italians and others have expressive gestures too."

He continued walking. "What you saw there was born from centuries of subjugation." He said that Indians become flailing cartoon figures when angered. "It's very undignified."

Later, in his living room—darkened by the curtains—while sipping sherry and puffing on his wine-scented cigarillo, he described how much he abhorred religious rituals. It was a hot evening and yet he was wearing his argyle sweater. He related an account of an officiating pundit who took his pet cat to religious functions because he lived alone and did not want to leave the animal behind. "In a short time, hissing strays were fetched for all the village pujas." He explained that in peasant societies, wars were fought over traditions that began, not from divine injunctions, but from simple acts of expediency. According to him, the religion of our ancestors, neutered by illiterate con men over the centuries, mirrored the country from which it sprang in the gradual loss of purpose. Astrological imperatives, magical mantras, worshipping of rats and snakes. He surprised me by saying that he, too, had been "corrupted" and it took a while before he had the space to see all of this properly. "I needed distance," he told me and I recalled my father's caustic observation of him.

This image of a young boy standing apart and contemptuously observing everything stuck, and I struggled to maintain my favourable impression of Mitra. A few days later, while I was varnishing his desk, he glanced up from his newspaper. "The thing that frightens these slackers the most is a perfect world where they have nothing to protest about."

He was reading about a downtown protest. I told him, "But the world is not perfect."

Mitra said nothing for a while, but when I was getting ready to leave, he intoned in his hybrid accent, interrupted with long pauses, that most activism was motivated by self-interest and was often used to propel laggards and tricksters to the front. I mentioned global warming as an example of activism forcing awareness of a critical problem.

"That is why I have no children, you see."

I noticed he would often conclude his arguments with a personal illustration.

Over the following days, he was provoked by some article or

the other to broadly condemn some group. "These brown fellas from Asia, they are always at each other's throats. What they don't see is that every online slur they direct at their perceived enemy is viewed in the wider community as also applying to themselves. Cutting their own necks." He chuckled as if he was imagining severed throats. Another day he said that when Blacks talk about racism, they are talking only about racism against Blacks. I tried to explain that this was so because of the magnitude of their suffering. "People make their lives," he said as if that was all there was to it. It was useless arguing with him. During an evening walk, he glanced at an Asian family and informed me that Asians looked down and distrusted anyone darker than themselves with the same ferocity with which whites viewed them. "They complain about upward racism not downward."

I found those casual opinions bothersome, so I informed him that while they might apply to his generation, mine was more forward-thinking.

This was a mistake because the following days he lectured me about millennials like me forming all our opinions from Facebook and drowning opposing views on Twitter. "There is too much vulgarity on display," he said. "This is how people now distinguish themselves."

This became his theme over the following days. I avoided him in the mornings when he was usually provoked by whatever he had read in the newspapers. In the evenings, during our walks, his mood shifted and he would point out a particular shrub or architectural oddity. He had an eye for detail and his descriptions made these objects and plants far more interesting than they should be. Later in the evening, while he was sipping his sherry and smoking, as he read one of his magazines, his criticisms, on the surface, seemed more general and reflective. Once, when he was commenting on the persuasive power of social media, he told me, “Whenever I think of Facebook, I think of Iago whispering into Othello’s ear.”

A few days later, when I walked up the basement steps, I saw Mitra gazing at a tiny mouse caught in a trap. I knew he was a vegetarian and claimed to be sickened by the sight of gristle and bloody bones so I asked if he wanted me to dispose of it. When he did not answer, I took the trap, trying not to look at the crushed rodent, placed it in a bag, and sent it down the garbage chute. “I have been looking at it twitching all morning,” he said when I returned. “It should not have been reborn as a rat. How is your job search?”

That week I redoubled my search for a job, which would enable me to move into my own place. I stripped down my resume; and one month after my arrival I got a job as a packer in a furniture factory. I expected Mitra to unleash some sneering comment, but he was surprisingly positive. “Some of you fellas come up here and expect to be installed straightaway in a fancy office. Do you know that my first job was as a porter? It allowed me to monitor people, you see. All the furtive dalliances,” he said, with a satisfied smile, his nostrils flattening. As he went on, I thought of him observing the twitching rodent. And for the first time, I realized he may have been also watching me from behind his magazines.

“I can get an apartment now,” I told him hurriedly.

“Certainly. We each need our independence.”

One day on our walk, during my last week at his place, he diverted us to an unfamiliar street. He walked more stylishly than usual, twisting his wrist so his cane struck the ground at an angle. When we got to the streetcar stop, he began to nod as if he were silently humming a song. When we boarded the streetcar, he hurried over to the single empty seat next to a large and florid woman, who immediately grabbed her grocery bags tighter and shifted away from him. At the next stop, she moved to another seat. Mitra was gazing out of the window.

When we got off, I mentioned the florid woman's action, and he told me, rather cheerfully, "Welcome to the new world."

"Were you not offended?"

He chuckled softly like someone watching a funny movie in a crowded cinema. "These are people at the bottom of the ladder. It gives them a little pleasure to feel there are others lower down, you see. Most of the people you meet here will be like this. *Classe inférieure*. Ah, we have arrived." Before us was a small red brick house with a steeply pitched roof and two front windows partially hidden by some kind of shrub. "There is a park at the end of the block," he said, briskly walking up the three stone steps. "I should be an hour or so."

I sat on the park bench and wished I had brought along a book. I looked up and saw that the clouds were not ragged and astir as those on the island but compact and higher in the sky, so that they seemed stationary. An old couple wearing light coats was sitting on a nearby bench gazing at a row of trees with knobby leaves. It was the end of September and a little ruffle of breeze, like a dying gasp, gently swept the treetops and all at once I missed the chaos of the island. The wild weather, the jumble of green shades, the cacophony of voices, the smell of rotting fruits, even the parasitic vines that strangled everything in their path. I wondered if Mitra had felt this way during his first months here.

I thought of his forgiving explanation about the streetcar episode and I considered whether I, too, would soon fall into the habit of enduring a shuttered and halfway life. But perhaps Mitra was always this way. I recalled his earlier assertion that he had "escaped the island." An hour later, I arrived at the red bungalow, and at the same time Mitra walked down the steps. A curtain shifted, and I saw a woman, her hair white, watching us. She reminded me of the tragic attic-dwelling women of some British novels.

"You are punctual," Mitra told me. "I cannot stand tardiness. It's a veil that hides more serious vices." As we approached the streetcar, I mentioned the woman gazing out, and he told me, casually, that it was his wife. He glanced at me and added, "She is suffering from nerves, you see. Bad business. We could not live together. Ah, there is the streetcar." He said nothing in the streetcar, where we sat together, but later, while he was sipping his sherry, I told him that I had not been aware of his marriage. He crossed his legs and flapped his magazine. "It was expected of me."

"What happened?"

Now he peered from behind his magazine. I could not tell if he was annoyed. "It petered out." I decided to leave it there, but as I was getting ready to head to my basement quarter, he added, "She could not understand my needs. Which reminds me . . . tomorrow I am taking you out. Good night."

Because of his frequent claim that vulgarity was a "gateway vice" that unleashed sloth and hypocrisy, I was surprised when our destination turned out to be Zanzibar, an old, dank strip joint. He sat quietly, his arms folded, and in the gloom he might well have been asleep. He commented on breast sizes and "deforested vaginas." The way he said *vaginas*, stretching it out, made me think of phosphorescent anemones. He revealed that in his younger days he would visit that joint during ladies' night and I wondered if he was about to reveal a deep secret. "I would go just before closing when the women were all fevered and readied by the events. *Then* I would swoop." I couldn't imagine him swooping, no matter how readied the women were. He spoke loudly, embarrassing me. "These women are doing God's work. It's a pity they get so little respect. Fine, fine specimens." As I listened to him describing the women and drawing concerned glances, I realized that not only was Mitra indifferent to the impression he created but he revelled in shocking people. "Nowadays, I am just a spectator," he exclaimed. “The wood is in a state of semi-retirement, you see.”

I was relieved to finally get my own apartment. Mitra’s view of the world, while interesting at first, had gradually worn me down. And because I was indebted to him, I had tried not to be argumentative. I sometimes felt that all his reading and his intelligence served one purpose—to verify his belief that hardship and suffering were self-induced. Always attentive and rigorous, he observed the afflicted as if he were studying an insect. Lacking was any sympathy.

When I was packing my stuff, I saw in his wastepaper basket the two bottles of pickled fruits my mother had sent him. I believe he left them there so I would notice. I asked if the fruits were perhaps too bitter. He smiled in his predatory manner, lips downturned and nostrils flattening. “I have no use for them.” He went to his Morris chair, crossed his legs, and lit a cigarillo. “You should take them with you.”

My new apartment had mold stains in the washroom and cobwebs on the ceiling and the carpet smelled of wet dog but for the first time in my new country I felt completely free. I visited Mitra twice during the first month. He called about the dripping in his kitchen sink and a week later about shifting his buffet stuffed with vintage trivets and gold-stemmed teacups. Both tasks were simple, and I suspected he really wanted to chat with someone. During my second visit, I told him truthfully that I could not come as often, if I got the extra shifts for which I had applied. He chuckled and went back to his newspaper as I exited his door.

He called each weekend to update me on his newest grievance. Our conversations began and ended in the same manner. He would complain about something, refer to an offending article, and he would then hang up abruptly. Once he mentioned that discrimination towards brown people was becoming normalized. He asked nothing of me, and I was thankful for this. I did not want to reveal that I had enrolled in an evening class and formed a relationship with a smart and attractive woman from Iran and we were thinking of moving into a better apartment. Mitra was suspicious of easy progress and he believed there was always some subterfuge involved in upward mobility.

It was easier to deal with him from a distance, free from obligations. I could easily have despised him—and there were moments when I did. What intrigued me was the puzzle of an educated, well-read man so easily given to petty prejudices. He was a paradox: he did not have the expected badges of privilege I associated with his pronouncements nor was he fighting to preserve a fading hierarchy or hankering over the good old days. Although his criticisms were routinely directed against the set-upon, no one escaped his gaze. He once told me that people who talked about the sophistication or the generosity of this country had never stepped out of the city into the small rural towns. And another time, "You must have noticed by now that while this place has an immaculately designed exterior, the interior is littered with dilapidated furniture." I had no idea what he meant until he added, "Corruption by the elites. Shrinking middle class. No corporate accountability. Poverty and homelessness." His views on religion were surprisingly progressive. He believed that inequality in primitive societies arose with the building of the first temples and he scorned those whose fealty to a divine being superseded every other loyalty. Once he told me, "Everyone here talks about moderation and nuances and all these fancy terms until it's their community which is threatened. Then the knives are out."

Many of his magazines were published in America and he remarked once that all great societies were brought down by a leader who, though despicable, mirrored the vices of his subjects. I wondered whether his scattershot misanthropy gave him a peculiar insight into the unfolding of tragedies and sometimes

I imagined him sipping his sherry in his gloomy living room, magazines on his lap, enlivened by the world turning on itself.

But I had my own world to see to. Engagement, pregnancy, miscarriage, the temporary closure of the furniture factory because of dwindling orders, the completion of my evening classes, and the search for another job. Over the following months, I replied into his voicemail only when I knew he would be out for his evening walk but his calls kept coming. One weekend, my fiancée asked me why I was ignoring someone who had assisted me after my arrival and I found myself struggling to explain Mitra's amused yet scathing view of the world. "You should telephone him." She mentioned the importance of familiar faces in an unfamiliar land and I knew she was right.

That night I called, and I was shaken by his hoarse, rattling voice. I asked if he was okay and he said he had seen enough of this world and was prepared to move on. "Those who have exited are far more interesting than the lot they have left behind. I do not belong here." I felt a surge of guilt and told him about my engagement and my work situation and my worry about whether my life here would match the one I had left behind. I heard his raspy, uneven breathing and wanted to apologize for bothering him with my problems, but he told me, "There are no new beginnings and neat endings. These are the delusions of desperate people wishing to move on to unencumbered lives." He cleared his throat. "Migrants never decloak themselves of their anxieties," he said, sounding more like the Mitra I knew. "They believe they can swing, like on a hammock, between two places. Everything must come to a stop, you see." I promised I would visit him soon.

Eleven days later, he was hospitalized and after a week on a ventilator, he passed away. I was informed of this and his upcoming funeral by a call from a woman who revealed that he did not want to be troubled by mourners. I was the only person apart from her he wished to be present. I assumed the caller was the woman he had visited in the small red bungalow with two front windows.

Apart from the Covid-mandated plexiglass barrier, the other restrictions at the funeral were entirely Mitra's. We were the only mourners and there was no eulogy. The woman, who was frailer than I had judged from that glance at her window close to a year earlier, had her hands clasped behind her back as she gazed down at Mitra. She was swaying slightly as if listening to a jazz pianist. When she slipped off her mask following the cremation, her thin compressed lips suggested sharp and alert eyes but after she removed her sunglasses, her expression conveyed tempered disinterest. For the briefest of moments, she reminded me of Mitra and I wondered at the battles they may have had.

While we were walking out, she asked, "I understand you stayed with Mitra for a couple of months. What was that like?"

"Six weeks. He explained this country to me."

"I bet he did." She seemed to be awaiting my response and when I said nothing, she continued, "He was the keenest observer of human nature I knew, but it was a double-edged sword."

"In what way?"

"You cannot fully observe a world from which you are absent. Mitra's phrase, when he was recovering from his nervous breakdown."

"I didn't know of that. He never mentioned it."

"He wouldn't do that now, would he?" She glanced at her watch, put on her shades, and lightly dusted her wrist. She took her time, a stylish, self-aware woman, and I imagined she and Mitra, both young and attractive, as a normal couple. Then she told me, "When I first got to know him, he shocked me by saying that people like him, denied any real power, are forced to be judgemental. Inadequacy parading as strength was how he put it. He said he saw his deformities with a clarity that wounded him deeply. Mit spoke like that, you know. Even during our . . . private moments."

The abbreviated name sounded unexpectedly affectionate, and I asked, "Will you miss him?"

She seemed surprised. I could see her thinking of a response. "It's too early to say." As she walked away, she added, "He would have given you a far better response."

When I got to our apartment, my fiancée asked about the funeral and I admitted I was glad I took her advice. My conversation with his wife—or ex-wife, I am not certain—though brief, had given me a truer insight into Mitra. His criticisms of particular groups—with whom he was tied either by culture or geography—was really a criticism of himself. His indifference was a pose, like the pose of a little boy standing by the road, refusing to join his family. My father was right, though he couldn't see that both sides of this halfway Indian were in constant battle.

The Second Life

I can recall clearly the view from the train window as I received the call. Slouched on the ground at the edge of a frozen pond just before Rouge Valley was a lone figure, a lanky man in a battered beige coat and hat. Before him was a scatter of seagulls on an oval rock, behind which stretched a wooded section of forlorn white pines and trembling aspens. The scene is fixed in my mind—the man's posture suggesting age and uneasiness—yet all I can remember from that five-minute call was my sister's declaration that my father's death was necessary.

As the train passed the nuclear plant in Pickering and the row of stately windmills along the shore, I reflected on my parents' visit to Ajax five years earlier. I had taken my father for a walk along the waterfront. He liked the arrangement of the trees, the handy benches, and the intersecting trails, and as someone who had spent his entire life on an island, he was drawn to the calming ripple of water and the hollow sound of wind streaking through the overlooking woodland. Whenever he saw an inscription on a plaque, he would pause to read the words aloud.

When he was a primary-school principal on the island, he would talk often about Canada. The current points of emigration from the island were America and England and I assumed my father's singular interest was because he had attended a high school and later an associated teachers' college founded and administered by Presbyterian missionaries from Nova Scotia and New Brunswick. His time at both institutions had been enjoyable, and it was difficult to imagine this quiet, almost melancholy man, so studious and meticulous, falling into the college tradition of pranks and mischief. During the drive to and from school in his Cortina, he would relate vague snippets about sneaking alcohol into the dorm, and although my siblings and I awaited some elaboration, it never came. The school trips were the only times he really spoke with us; like most village principals of that era, he was frequently busy in the evenings drafting letters, organizing petitions, and administering rural associations. At his desk, his thin and dark face always carried a frown. Making announcements, he spoke in the measured style of someone who, not naturally gifted as a speaker, adopted a carefully rehearsed script.

And that was the voice he used in reading the inscriptions, the words crisp and metallic on that nippy fall afternoon in Ajax. He was more talkative than I remembered, certainly more than during his previous visits. His steps were shorter but whenever I slowed my pace, he would hasten until he was just ahead. He stopped on a bridge to look at a pair of swans in the distance, the bounce of the waves and the lilt of their necks making it appear as if they were performing a glissade choreographed for us. My father must have been thinking precisely this, because he began to wave an arm like an inspired conductor.

A passerby might have imagined some playfulness in the little pantomime, but my father's face was as serious as when he stood before the school assembly. And with that serious expression, he started to sing, "Goosey, Goosey Gander where shall I wander? . . . " I was startled, because at the last line, he lifted his leg as if he was thinking of jumping from the bridge.

"What are you doing?" I asked him.

"I want to swim with the swan."

I tried to hide my alarm and hurried him towards the forested lot.

"Bears?" he asked a few minutes later.

"No bears here. Just raccoons and squirrels."

"I had a little squirrel once. It used to sleep here." He pointed to his pants pocket.

"Was it tame?"

"It ran away." He repeated the statement in a distressed manner. A short while later, he spotted a squirrel skittering along a willow tree and he shouted, "Come, boy. Stop combing that tree." He held his pocket open. "Come back here." Now he laughed as he ran towards the willow. I followed him, worried. I had never seen this playful side before and I remember thinking that he had certainly mellowed with age. But there was also a maniacal quality to his playfulness, as if he might lose control any minute. I inquired if he was cold and he looked at his hands. I asked him once more, when I noticed he was rubbing his knuckles, and he shook his head.

Some distance away, a green-winged teal was circling a red oak. I followed him to the tree. He stood in the old principal's manner, his hands clasped against his back, looking at the birds. Just beyond the oak was a line of maples, the leaves a scandalous red. I have always felt that for a newcomer to this place, accustomed to one or two measly seasons, it is the bewitching foliage of autumn rather than the snow or ice of winter that shocks. The photographs and movies that depict the bleakness of winters so well can never convey the vividness of the variegated leaves sweeping the sky and jazzing up the ground.

We stood there for almost five minutes before he started

drawing circles in the air. He seemed a bit frustrated, as if he were searching for the words to describe the scene within his circle. Eventually, he jabbed his finger in the direction of the trees and then to his heart. I tried to determine whether his gesture indicated devotion, admiration, or ownership. "Do you like it?" I asked him.

"Very," he said. "All of it."

"All? Even the chill?" I asked provokingly.

He seemed to be contemplating his answer. Eventually, he provided clarification to another question, one from half a century earlier, when he would talk mysteriously about a lost opportunity to move to Canada. And suddenly, the unfamiliar hesitancy of the prior half-hour or so was gone. His memory, so stuttering a few minutes earlier, seemed stabilized as he described an event that occurred when he was a young man. We neared Pickering, the occasional dog walkers the only signs that we were not in an abandoned woodlot. He walked with short pattering steps, unstable sometimes, but he did not want to turn back even when I mentioned the cold or his exhaustion. On our way to the house, I felt this had been our longest conversation for as long as I could recall. During the three days prior to his departure, he was quiet, and I wondered if the revelation of his long-closeted pain had drained him.

Four years passed. I heard accounts of his behaviour from my siblings. I tried to distance myself from the stranger they described. Sometimes I held our conversation of that frigid autumn evening as a sort of countervailing narrative to the stories relayed over the phone.

That afternoon on the train, the tenor of the call was different; and during the flight to the island, I felt a rush of panic. The minute the plane left the ground, the emails and telephone conversations I had tried to tune out came rushing back into my mind. As my father's memory froze and splintered, leaving shards to which he desperately clung, he had grown increasingly frustrated and petulant, even towards my mother, the only person he could now recognize. I heard of his dissembling in conversations with people he could no longer place, his little chats with television characters, the time he wandered out of the gate and was found on a lonely teak-lined road a mile away by one of his former pupils.

Some of these mishaps had the clumsy jokiness of a B-movie and at first, my sister would laugh when she was relating one or the other of his blunders. But as he lost the ability to make simple connections, he grew by turn morose and hostile. Each evening, at the approach of darkness, he asked why his parents (long-dead) had stopped visiting and either cried or grew vehement when an explanation was offered. Sometimes, he would swipe away the food from the table and in the nights my mother was awakened by him rattling the wrought-iron gate. Once, she told my sister that whenever she got accustomed to one of my father's altered personalities, he entered another. She said it was like watching someone die in installments.

Another image, no less stark, came to mind following the conversations and emails. Black stars in a white sky; the mind strains to the past and to jerky memories of youth and childhood while the body accelerates towards debility. I wondered whether it was like being forced to make a simultaneous journey in opposite directions. At times, I tried to imagine the anguish of someone accustomed to routines and schedules, glimpsing as through a frosted window all of this slipping away. The moments of lucidity, growing more infrequent each week, might provide a jerking reprieve from the opacity but it must also inflict some consciousness of what had been reeled off into darkness.

All of this was conjecture on my part. So far away, I had struggled to understand his memory impairment, but I had no precedent and I sometimes reflected whether the old men and women I had glimpsed as a boy, staring out of their windows, disappearing for long periods, may have been similarly afflicted. At the time, they just appeared crazy.

Crazy. A childish word that should have simplified his condition. But in a community where age was associated with wisdom, my father's condition—to his family, at least—resisted this easy reduction. Whenever I heard from my sister of him dredging up slices of his own distant past and seating relatives from one generation next to friends from another, I imagined his memories as pieces of old furniture strewn around, in a space without any enclosing rooms as signifiers. And worse, everything shifted around each night in a cruel joke. I thought of him this way: as constantly reeling from little pranks. But he was still remarkably strong, my siblings assured me. Then began the fainting spells, the ministrokes that left him weaker and even more confused. During the last episode, he had banged his head against the sharp edge of a table.

I had resisted returning; I wanted to remember him as a whole person; as the man who, five years earlier, stepping carefully over the fallen leaves at the waterfront, had revealed that on the week of his graduation from the teachers' college, the principal had journeyed to the house of my grandparents with an untenable proposal. Likely, the gaps in my father's memory had already begun but he had related this story in the manner of a writer, beginning with a description of the lean principal and my stocky grandfather. The trip must have been about four hours or so on muddy and gravelly roads and my father described the encounter in the front gallery between these two formidable men, natural adversaries, one a Presbyterian missionary, who in the fashion of the time, viewed the rituals practised by the country Indians as superstitions to be wiped out, and the other a Brahmin priest whose function was to protect and perpetuate these practices. Although the meeting was polite, my father explained that midway in the conversation, he was summoned by my grandfather.

For a while, my father seemed lost in reflection, and I asked, "What did he say to you?"

He stopped and, as if pointing to an invisible stranger, thundered phrases in Hindi. I asked him to translate, and he said that my grandfather had asked why he was trying to create enmity between two strangers and taint the older man's role as a gracious host. I could not understand where this story was leading and I put my hand on my father's shoulder to slow his pace. What was the purpose of the principal's visit? I asked.

"He wanted to take me away, boy."

"Take you where?"

"To New Brunswick for a course in theology." He explained that it would be preparation for his induction as a Reverend in the Presbyterian Church.

"And what did my grandfather say?"

"After he quarrelled with me in Hindi, he told the man in English that he was sorry that his stupid son had behaved so foolishly. 'He could have saved you this long trip,' he said. They had dinner together, and that was the end of that. Neither of them brought it up again during the dinner." I wanted to ask my father if he had been disappointed by the outcome of the meeting, but I kept quiet. We continued walking and a few minutes later, he told me, "Everything happens for a reason." He seemed dissatisfied with his response and gestured for me to stop. When I did, he told me, "In my next life."

"What will happen in your next life?"

He made the circle and pointed to his chest once more. And on that fall evening, as he described this person he would be reborn as, I realized that his descriptions did not match his father but the principal of his teacher's college, the man who had come to a remote village with an unwieldy proposal. If the conversation had been with someone other than my father, I would have laughed at the silliness, but I felt a little nudge of pity for him, carrying this disappointment for such a long time.

Perhaps there is something about the disequilibrium of journeys that rouses the memory. On the plane, I recalled every detail of our conversation along the waterfront in Ajax. It made me apprehensive but at the house, where I had grown up, everyone seemed relaxed. At the gate, a sister greeted me and asked if I had heard a newborn baby crying during my trip. I could not understand at first, then I remembered the old belief that life is never truly snuffed out but swiftly and infinitely passes along.

I spent four days on the island. In my father's room on the main floor, his old closet stood close to a window overlooking a grove of crisscrossing bamboo. The original mirror with its diagonal crack had been replaced, and the handles were not the brass knuckles I knew. But the interior was as I remembered it. On the upper shelves were an assortment of pens, pencils, stencils, and pots of ink in a brass jar, and cufflinks and tie clips and an old wristwatch in another. On the middle shelf, his ties hung from a hook beneath two felt hats. On the lowest shelf were faded letters in his elegant and practised handwriting and a few charcoal renditions of pictures he had copied from the *West Indian Reader*, mostly by John Constable, and photographs that I had seen close to half a century earlier. They had held no meaning then but now I recognized as a port in Halifax and a view of the Saint John River in Fredericton. I thought of the speeches, liberally sprinkled with quotations, that he made at his school; standing before his closet now, I realized that he had been imitating the works of others, to which he owed much of his success. He had been a noted principal but his ambitions had been capped by repetition, ritual, and imitation. It was a life constantly in abeyance.

After the cremation, as I headed towards the airport, I observed the bulldozers parked next to the excavated zones, the neatly cut box-drains, the diverse styles of houses, and the tinkering and additions that still retained hints of the older cantilevers and railings. And ironically, all these postponements and abandonment gave the impression of a place constantly in motion, bending to every new influence. I thought of my father's closet, undisturbed for so long, housing all the little signs of the man he wanted to be. If not this life, then some other.

So

The woman died in a hospital in Florida a day after the cardiologist assured her four children that her surgery was successful, and they would now have the mother they desired. Following that diagnosis, a daughter, relieved, returned to Trinidad. Another daughter remained at the hospital where she had spent the last three nights at her mother's bedside. And it was this daughter, overcome with grief and anger, who sent the WhatsApp message: *she's gone*. A son, the eldest of the four children and living in Canada, his suitcase packed, the taxi already called, assumed she had been discharged early from the hospital. Still, he was disturbed by the brevity and ambiguity of the message. Five minutes later, his sister called from Florida, saying he should cancel his trip to Florida and instead go to Trinidad. From her voice, he already knew, but it was a shock nonetheless hearing her say, "For the funeral."

On his flight to Trinidad somewhere above Cape May, he fell asleep. He dreamed he was on the way to see his mother, and then in the manner of dreams, he was in the rear seat of a car driven by his sister. Both were assuring their mother that her worries about the surgery were baseless. He was jolted awake by a surge of turbulence, and for a minute or so, he was disoriented by the dream and the shuddering plane and a moment of eerie stasis, and it was only when he looked through the windows at the Caribbean islands winking like shattered glass that the hope was broken. Perhaps it was the drowsy aftermath of the dream or the way the plane felt suspended in a gloved hand above the glinting islands, but at that moment, he realized that it had been his mother's fable-like descriptions half a century earlier of other lands that first put in his head the notion of emigration. He was surprised, because such revelations did not come easily to him. Soon he heard the captain's voice, and his mind turned to the tableau beneath.

When he was a boy, he had gone to the airport to fetch uncles and aunts for the funerals of his grandparents, and he always wondered what these expats—which is how he thought of them—had been thinking during their flights. He himself had returned the year before for his father's funeral, and despite his fears then, everyone had been upbeat and even relieved. Now, the sister who met him at the airport looked stunned.

Not so the villagers who swung into action, cutting bamboo, building a tent, comforting the family. Each hour someone, usually an older woman, dropped by to express disbelief and to inquire about the body's arrival. And the children shared the news from their sister in Florida: The body had been transferred from the hospital in Jacksonville to the funeral home. From the funeral home it would be sent to Atlanta. From Atlanta to Miami. A week stretched into two. The plane had to be a specific size to carry caskets, they had been told. The Trinidadian embassy had to sign documents to repatriate the remains. There were other delays, and their sister's voice sounded shrunken and wrung each day, even when she was insisting it would be pointless for anyone to journey to Florida to help with the repatriation. And now the villagers shifted their sympathies to this daughter, a cancer survivor who was overseeing all this.

And the children and the other mourners waited and waited. In the late evenings, after the devotional services in the tent, when the place was cooler, they gathered in a gazebo wreathed with sinuous wild orchids where the woman had liked to sit and look out at the hummingbirds, and beyond, a field of battling marigolds and zinnias and hibiscus their mother had planted. No one knew what she might have been musing about during those periods, but the group of children and women from the village tried to match her view. They drew comfort from each other, and from the softness of the fading day, the harsh light muted, the sharp chiselled colours so unsuited to grief.

It's hard to believe she is really gone, the village women said brightly as if they didn't believe it. One evening, a woman claimed that the previous day, just as she was thinking of the dead woman, she turned on the radio and heard a song favoured by her. Another woman professed to see her shape in a flickering candle. Yet another heard her voice in the medley of assembling parakeets. Someone had smelled her favourite perfume. Her closest friend, a woman in her eighties, was silent but then one night she, too, said she had received a message. We should continue with our groups. And we should keep the men out. They will spoil everything.

Soon the village women departed to tend to other obligations until just the children were left. They should have been tired, but they were energized by remorse, a crazed energy that rippled beneath the bowed heads and the clasped fingers and set lips. Sometimes, there were brief thunderstorms that descended with a malevolent fierceness, and the children watched gnarled rivulets pattering on the asphalt yard and leaping into the drains. They smelled the tangy aroma of wet grass and pitch and looked at rainflies cascading around the bulbs and falling into the yard, washed away, their tiny gauzy wings beating frantically before they were torn off the bodies. Then the lizards came.

In the silence of the night, they tried to circumvent sadness by thinking of what might have made their mother unique among the other women of her generation who had surrendered their lives to their husbands and children. Her own mother had died when she was twelve, and she was married five years later and brought into a house of strangers, nine in all. One evening, someone inquired of her father-in-law if they had acquired a new maid.

She never forgot those years; they marked her and made her. Often, she would relate to her young children stories so similar to the ones she told about her own life, it was hard to tell the difference. They all featured a downtrodden woman with a heart of gold. They were tragedies that seemed desultory and despairing, and the resolutions offered no real lessons. Many of her stories were Indian variations of *Beauty and the Beast*. The twist was that the beast revealed no hidden virtue to his victims. In time, though, the stories, told now to grandchildren, changed into morality plays demonstrating the strength of faith, persistence, and confidence. All her stories ended with, "So," her head turned to the side, her eyes looking to the floor, or what was beneath it. She contoured the syllable into an elongated pause that seemed flecked with hope and loneliness and acceptance. And the children never knew if that "So" was just emptiness, an echo of lost endings, or if it represented a promise of new beginnings.

One night during a moment of silence in the gazebo, the elder son tried to imagine her life like one of her stories. His sister asked what he was thinking of, and he recited, more or less, these words:

Once upon a time, there was a girl whose mother died in childbirth. She was taken from school to care for her family: her father, two older brothers, and a younger sister. She missed her friends at school and in the nights she cried herself to sleep about her broken dream of becoming a nurse. She grieved for her mother, who had taken her and her younger sister to the capital where they rode the tramcars and wandered around the botanical garden and marvelled at the castles and gingerbread houses. On their way back, she would warn her two children they should not say anything about their explorations to their strict and humourless father. Once she had taken the pair to the wharf, where families in suits accompanied by cardboard suitcases were staring anxiously at the huge ship about to dock. The girl, as she had done when she had viewed the gingerbread houses, dreamed of escape. So.

The son felt a slight relief in viewing her life as a fable where nothing was real, and gods pretended to be beggars and death was an accessory to the bigger play of the world. The group in the gazebo went silent for a while. They gazed around uneasily. The frogs in the distance croaked and belched. In the night, her flowers looked blue and ethereal and venous as if they had been plucked from another world. A sister felt a sudden chill and tightened her arms over her chest. This sister, a psychiatrist, wondered where her mother's body was and imagined her spirit floating around, trying to find its way home. Eventually, she said in a dead voice that their mother had wanted a simple funeral. Cremate me the next day, she had said. With no fuss. Just like your father's funeral.

Some nights, the children, their arms folded, moved to the tent, and they recalled sitting in the same spot a year earlier for their father's wake. Their moods had been light then; their father had been released from six or seven years of darkness. Now, the three children in Trinidad contrasted their mother's attitudes to their father's insecurities and mood swings, his stubbornness, his bind to tradition and fear of change, his emphasis on education. Once, the daughter said, "She never taught us anything directly." They looked at each other and considered that revelation. The daughter elaborated, "Remember her story of the Muslim neighbours who brought food for them every evening when her mother died? She wanted us to figure out things, like she did."

The children, in their fifties and early sixties, were old enough to know that curiosity in women of their mother's generation was actively discouraged by the men, their self-appointed guardians who cited archaic, convoluted conventions. Some women, too, gradually disfigured into silence, saw this inquisitiveness as a precursor to promiscuity, and joined the parade of persecutors. Now the adult children were led to conflicts and tensions, and they recalled their father's silent and sullen moments. They were relieved there had been no outright quarrels, but they did not wish to go further because arriving at a fuller understanding of one parent would likely tarnish the other.

"They were the opposite of each other," the daughter said. Her two brothers considered the differences.

She would laugh at silly little things and, following his Alzheimer's, her face would light up mischievously when he said something foolish and unexpected. Before his illness, their father made jokes that no one understood and which were only revealed as jokes when he laughed soundlessly. It was easy to mistake this eruption for sobbing, and in his later years, as his memories receded, even his family could not tell the difference. She was often irritated with her husband's altered personality, and the children now wondered whether it was a residual bitterness for her speechless years. Perhaps she, too, might have seen this because after each moment of irritation, she would sit at the table with him and talk playfully. Still, she was not a forgiving woman. She once told her elder son that people who apologized were cowards and hypocrites and everyone was honest only when they were enraged. That is when their true colours showed, she added. This son recalled dimly his mother's tears and anger during that admission, and he was brought back to what she had endured.

This time he kept these thoughts to himself.

In a place of many rivers and a fierce sun, there lived a young woman who took breaks from her chores by looking out of the window at the egrets dipping their giraffe necks into the muddy water across the road and the butterflies, caught by sudden gusts, roused from the marigolds in the front yard. Sometimes, she dreamed in a childish way of someone suddenly appearing to take her away from poverty. He would be handsome like the heroes from Hindi movies and gentle and live in an estate with animals roaming around. Her calf, Munna, would be there, too. One day she spotted a car in the driveway. From the car emerged a young man. He was thin and very dark and dressed too formally to be one of the villagers who sometimes visited her father. He was examining the mud on his tires when he suddenly looked up. He was nothing like the heroes in her stories. She pulled the curtains angrily.

And so it happened that at the edge of the forest, there was a new wife who found herself in a house much like the one she had dreamed of. It overlooked a field of bananas and cocoa, and there were seven bedrooms. But in each of these bedrooms was an in-law. Her sisters-in-law and brothers-in-law were her age or a few years younger, and they were all at school. So she found herself once more tending to a family, cooking, sweeping, washing. This arrangement had been an unwritten law for centuries, but this young wife had witnessed too many broken dreams. One day, she took her two-year-old son to her father's place. She was pregnant at the time, and from habit she sat at the window looking out, pretending not to hear her father's entreaties. One morning, she saw a car pulling into the muddy driveway and a slim dark man in a tie stepping out.

The son tried to add balance to this picture. Was she, perhaps, luckier than she had imagined, married to a man who, though he was conservative and timid, came from a relatively wealthy family that understood the value of education? Did she glean something fraught but indispensable from her own mother during the trips to the capital for tramcar rides? In a colour-obsessed society, did her striking paleness give her undue confidence?

And so it went. While they waited, uncertain grief opened the levers to everything they knew or thought they knew about a woman whose body was a few thousand miles away. They desperately wanted their remembrances to be pleasant, but their mother's voice was too strong. Once, a stray dog, old and sick, had slunk away to the corner of the house, refusing attention, and she had told her disturbed daughter: That is what animals do when they are old and dying. They look for a corner because they want to be left alone to die in peace. That daughter also recalled her mother's objections to the surgery that took her life, saying she was eighty years old and could manage with her old defective valve. And she had closed her eyes as if she did not want to hear the empty beat of her children's optimism. "Look at us here," the daughter said awkwardly, clearing her throat. "Struggling to understand somebody after their has life passed away."

A few minutes later, the elder son said, "All in all, she had a good life."

The other son, not usually talkative, brought up an article he had read that tried to prove an average person with food, clothing, and accommodation could be just as happy as a millionaire. His siblings tried to understand the connection between their mother's death and this arbitrary hypothesis. Perhaps, he was trying to say anyone could be happy but his description stroked the unease that had been bubbling beneath the surface of that meeting. They had all persuaded her to go into surgery; and in the moments of silence they stretched their roles, their complicities. In their minds, she was still alive, looking on with disapproval at the betrayal. And in the dead stillness of the nights, they all sensed her. She could not be properly unlatched because of unfulfilled matters. A priest who had dropped by to remind the children of complicated rituals made matters worse, for he spoke of the soul as if it were a gradually dripping box or a sieve clotted with particles. Some of the children sensed that regret would hover around long after the grief had passed.

Finally news arrived that the body was on its way; finally a cremation could be scheduled. Once more, the place was abuzz with activity. The children in Trinidad were relieved that the weight of abeyance might now be eased. A flawed relief took hold, and they rushed here and there, offering to help but mostly getting in the way of villagers seasoned in this rite of passage. Go to the funeral home, the villagers told them gently. And wait for the body. And it was there they saw the sister who had been travelling with her dead mother for over two weeks. Her face was blank; the life seemed have been sucked out of her bones. The brother from Canada who had not seen her in a year was shocked by her bald head, her cheekbones, her dull eyes. Yet it was she who calmed the other daughter and the two sons. They saw within her a deep rage, and they said comforting words to her, and she nodded, and the act of comforting, so inadequate, released piecemeal whatever had lodged in their souls. And this sister, always practical, asked about the priests and the village women and the tent.

The night before the cremation a terrible storm roiled the southern half of the island. At the home of the dead woman, the wind shrieked, and the trees danced, the tips of the tall bamboo bent and brushed the ground. On a nearby immortelle, the pendulous cornbird's nests convulsed before they were flung away. The children looked anxiously at the canvas flapping and billowing. A daughter thought of a raging spirit. When the storm passed, the canvas roof was bloated with water, and the poles tottered dangerously. The children stood on chairs with broom handles to disperse the pools of water on the canvas. "She is angry," the daughter who had returned from Florida said. She laughed suddenly, harshly, as if seeing the statement as ridiculous. And her practical side took over. Following the surgery, her mother had asked for a pen and paper and had written her last wishes. Most of what she had written had to do with the women's group.

"Who will deliver the eulogy?" this daughter asked. "It should be an honest representation of her life. She talked about the women's group till the end." She looked at the elder son, but his eyes were closed.

Once upon a time, there was a mother who, with the birth of each child felt she was sinking further into a life of hopelessness. Sometimes, she looked at her children and felt she should hoist all her dreams onto them. But at other times, she saw in them only the reflections of their father's face, and the dreams sputtered and died. Everything comes to an end, she thought. I must have committed some serious crime in a prior life. So, she waited for the end.

And when the woman was seventy-two years old, her husband, eight years her senior, was diagnosed with Alzheimer's. He was a former principal and had spent his retirement years heading committees of farmers and religious organizations. His wife, the woman who had given up on life, was pushed into these groups because the villagers liked continuity and because she had access to all his logbooks with carefully detailed expenditures.

But her passage was not easy. She did not possess her husband's gift for flattery and his forbearance. Some of the men who could not tolerate her forthright approach dropped out. These positions she replaced with women. Soon, all the committees were headed by women. By the time her husband died six years after his diagnosis, many of the men had returned. They sat in the back rows, folded their arms, and listened to their wives.

The crowd gathered in the tent on the day of the funeral followed this arrangement. Then the body arrived, and it looked nothing like the woman the children and the mourners remembered. The skin was dark grey, and the cheekbones seemed dislodged, so her nose appeared flattened, her eyes sunken, and her lips thinner. In death, every bit of her beauty that had provoked interest was taken away. The women who came up to sprinkle flowers pressed their lips against their *orhnis*, and their daughters turned away quickly. The elder son thought: this is a good thing because it will loosen my affection but his sister, the one who had stayed in Trinidad, was aghast at the thought that this image would be the last she would have of her mother, one she would always carry around. The daughter who had been with the body in Florida never took her eyes off the casket; the younger son avoided looking entirely.

When it was time for eulogies, the son who had seen a benefit to the shrivelled, mummified appearance tried to transpose this image to the entirety of her life. He listened to the eulogies, and he thought: my mother was no saint. Why are they deifying her? She had been struck by tragedies, but so had many other women of her generation. Some were decidedly more so. Yet, knowing all this, he was unexpectedly moved by the accounts. And when a woman said his mother had counselled her at a bad time and stopped to wipe her tears, he felt his own eyes burning.

The cremation site was on a hill shaded by mango trees and overlooked the ocean. From the hill, the green sea was veined with streams of mud that burst at a distance. Birds toiled in the sky and dipped into the silty overflow and flew away. Tiny grey crabs scuttled among the rinsed bones and litter on the shore. During her cremation, there was a loud explosion and a scatter of sparks. The pundit told the daughter who had travelled with the body, "That is her soul being released."

The younger son told him, "I think it's her pacemaker."

The pundit said, "Yes, she was a peacemaker. Your father was different."

The children glanced at each other, and for the first time in almost a month, they smiled.

And they hoped that the sight of their mother's body consumed by fire would in some small way end their attachment.

The tent was dismantled. The villagers resumed their lives. Most had pulled themselves out of poverty and were seasoned to the never-ending cycle of life and death. The children wished to be like that, but they had never suffered. Their mother had hidden them, protected them. Each believed her passing would irrevocably change their life. A son suspected his recent experiment with sobriety would end; his elder brother, an artist, confessed emotionally that his mother had always been the source of his inspiration; a daughter revealed that each morning she had planned her day's activities around her mother's schedule; the other one thought the strength to resist her illness, confounding her oncologist, was derived from a determination to take care of her mother. They understood their mother's time had come—a phrase uttered by the priest—and although they were practical in other matters, each felt that their world had changed. There was no passage back to easier times.

A sister suggested they all meet in the gazebo. During one gathering, the daughter who had been with her mother's body said, "Big old men and women still grieving for their *mummy*." They were glad it was she who had come up with this observation. And so, they began to think of the dozens of impoverished families bursting with motherless children, young women who had left toddlers and babies behind. They recounted—and were reassured by tragedy's reach. Death was everywhere; grief as raucous and variegated as the parakeets that skittered on the trees every morning. Perhaps one daughter had used this description to the son who lived abroad and who returned there a month after the funeral. In his adopted land, he felt cut off from this tropical grief that he envisaged as lush with memories and apparitions.

Mourning in the tropics is different, he once thought. It's effusive and unpredictable. He had been to three funerals in Canada, and they were muted, sombre affairs with weeks of rituals and ceremonies concentrated into two hours. In the tropics, funerals, like weddings, were prolonged, immersive spectacles. So, four months following the cremation, when one of his siblings called to talk of their mother, he wished to be left alone, to contemplate quietly, to draw circles around his depression. It's impossible to heal properly in a noisy crowd, he thought once, but he said nothing. For as long as he could remember, he had found religion to be interesting but absurd. And he had shuttered hysteria decades ago.

A year after the cremation, he returned to the island for a religious ritual. He had thought of skipping the trip, but had missed by a few hours seeing his mother alive, and he feared a similar situation was on the verge of repeating itself. During this flight, there were no dreams, and the plane was packed with noisy farm workers returning with money and stories. A man with his baseball cap tilted stylishly asked, "You was on a farm too?"

The question surprised him slightly, but he said, "A death."

"Ah," the man said sympathetically. "When is the funeral?"

"A year ago."

The son heard the other passenger fiddling with his pouch. The man retrieved a mint, plopped it into his mouth, and reclined his seat. But a few minutes later, he asked, "Father or mother?"

"Mother."

"It tough with mothers. So why you now going?"

"For a ceremony."

"Ah. She was religious?"

The son remembered dimly her stories from the *Mahabharata* about epic battles and sacrifices on a grand scale and warrior-women.

"She liked stories and fables," he told the passenger.

The passenger began to talk about Aesop and Hans Anderson and *soucouyants*. His voice from chewing was wet and slippery. The son looked out of the window at the swollen black sea. Once upon a time, he began . . . The passenger shifted closer to hear his muttering. The son tried again. Once upon a time, a woman had a daughter who never left her side . . .

"Is a story you making up? You remember how in school all the stories used to end with 'The monkey break his back for a piece of pommerac?' How yours going to end?"

"Not sure," he told the man. But another word spilled into his mind.

So.

Jahaji Bundle

Most of Raj's life in Canada was spent dreaming of the boisterous village he had memorized, house by house, so he was occasionally disoriented to awaken in chilly drafts or to numbing silences. In the meantime, his wife outgrew his reverence for a place she had hated and moved on to a new life, and his son increasingly distanced himself from a father he began to see as an anxious and reproachful custodian. Raj, in turn, viewed his family as ungrateful, not towards him but to their island. He noted how swiftly they had adopted other ways of speaking and dressing, and if he were not so tightened with dismay during these early months, he might have realized that he was angered less by these acts of assimilation than by the conviction that his family had refused to suffer with him. Because they did not share his regret, they were weak and shallow. Sometimes in conversations he would try to dredge up the folksy tones of the island, but he felt as if he was talking to strangers and he stumbled.

He was aware of how foolish he sounded whenever he expressed his disappointment. This realization roused him to angry outbursts and even more incoherence. He suspected his family were unimpressed—or worse, amused—by his garbled objections. So, a year and a half after they arrived in Canada, he decided to stay silent. He became a watchman. A silent witness to the daily transgressions. He watched as his wife departed with their daughter to Vaughn, where she had recently been offered a job. He watched as fellow supply teachers were granted long-term positions while his applications were routinely rejected. He watched as his son, who was forced to remain in the high-rise in Whitby because he had just started high school, joined a rock band, hung out with an insolent young woman, and returned late at night reeking of marijuana. He saw himself growing smaller and more irrelevant with each observation.

All of this Raj watched. And he compared. At his high school on the island, he had worn a uniform, returned home at an appointed time, and spent an hour cutting bundles of grass for the animals before he could join the family at the boxy cedar table for dinner. He received awards for oration and poetry which he proudly shared with his parents, and he was among the top five in his class every year. He made no decision without a blessing from his parents. He remembered the months spent studying for his A levels and he reconstructed this stressful period into little acts of contented sacrifices. The bumpy two-hour journey by bus to his school, the brutality of the teachers, the inconvenience of living with no electricity until he was fifteen, the regular water shortages, the inescapable meals from the breadfruit tree that hung over the swampy patch of dasheen in the back were each transformed in the same manner. Increasingly, these backward glances threw up visions of a paradise. Some part of him knew this was not real, but these fantasies latched onto him like an addiction, bestowing a torpor that momentarily dulled his rage.

It was always directed to his son, who reminded him of his failures. Sometimes he wished the boy would go to his mother's place. When his son did leave his place, the year he finished high school, the father forgot how often he had wished for this outcome and chalked the move to another act of ingratitude. At least now he was free to maintain his trysts with a fellow supply teacher at the Durham Board, but a few months later she told him she was enrolling at a divinity college in Toronto. "Making amends," she said with more passion than he could remember. "It's never too late." Remarkably, he was relieved; their relationship had been only physical and gradually he felt pinned down by the weekly routine.

The following year, his ex-wife was diagnosed with ovarian cancer. He had recently bought an old, dilapidated wartime house; his ex's condition appeared as an unnecessary disruption to the restoration he had planned. Twice he planned to visit her, but each time he got diverted to other destinations: once, to a farmer's market in Stouffville and then to the Alderville First Nation reserve. At the trading post, he purchased a dreamcatcher.

On the way back, Raj remembered a poem from his primary school. "There was an Indian who had known no change." He did not know—nor did the teacher explain—that these Indians were a different people. Close to the end of the poem, there was the line about "Columbus's doom-burdened caravels," but it was years before he understood the poem's stark meaning. As he passed the small towns—Welcome, Newtonville, Courtice—the tracts of farmland reminding him of the island's sugarcane fields—he resolved to make more of these countryside trips.

When he returned home, there were three messages on his home phone. They were from his daughter. His ex had passed away. She was sixty-one, four years younger than him. He had expected the disease to progress slowly. During her funeral service, he sat next to his daughter, and was surprised at her composure. She had not inherited this trait from him. Throughout the ceremony, he glanced around for his son, and only spotted him hurrying away at the end of the service.

Following his ex's death, Raj missed the island even more. He continued taking long drives in the Ontario countryside, hoping this time to displace his yearning with Canadian vistas. One evening, while walking through the White Pine Loop in Uxbridge, he remembered a stanza of a poem he had read in high school by the Chinese poet Li Po. "By the bamboo stream the last fragment of cloud/ Blown by the wind slowly scatters away." He recalled the strange word, *psithurism*, that described the sound of wind blowing through pine trees. This memory drew him to others, the chirks and hums of bamboo and teak, the fragrance of overripe guava and primrose, a picoplat's roulade, and the force of their recollection was so fierce that he knelt in the middle of the path to catch his breath. He put it down to a panic attack but his doctor sent him for a series of tests that pointed to a faltering heart.

Later in the week, Raj paid a visit to his son, who was renting in Parkdale. He planned on revealing his recent diagnosis, but the coldness on his son's face held him back. He would have told his daughter, but she was in Japan, teaching English. He began to dread the thought of dying alone, his undiscovered corpse rotting in his room. His health, which he had taken for granted, had now like everything else turned against him. The plan to renovate the wartime house was no longer possible. The week after his visit to his son, he dreamed there was a black snake, bloated and slippery, in his room. He somehow slung a rope around the serpent. In the dream, he abandoned the bedroom but each time he went upstairs he heard it thrashing. One night, the area, smelling of rotting flesh, was silent. He was about to open the door when he heard a subtle shifting beneath the bed.

He awoke from this dream as frightened as he had been two generations earlier of stories about *soucouyants* and *lagahoos* roaming the village. For three nights, he slept on the couch downstairs and each time he passed the bedroom on his approach to the toilet, he imagined the odour of rotting flesh. This is stupid, he thought. I am a sixty-six-year-old man. So he returned to the room. The first night there he awoke with a tightness in his chest and panicked, thinking it was the snake. He rushed out, dizzy and nauseous. He fell on his way to the toilet. When he recovered, light was already streaming through the window. He dressed carefully, as for a job interview, and drove to the hospital, ten minutes away. The following week, he had an angioplasty and a stent insertion.

His daughter arrived from Japan with a frail-looking boy. They were an odd couple, and he was surprised at how robust she appeared in her athletic clothes. The pair went for morning jogs and he was further astonished at how much he awaited their return, even their incomprehensible conversations. Ten days after her arrival, she told him she must report to her teaching job in Japan. She somehow managed to convince her brother to move in with their father, but each night when the boy left for work in Toronto, the father noticed his resentment at the obligation. His daughter's features and mannerisms reminded him of her mother, but he could see no familiarity in his son, no connection to him or his wife.

It seemed as if he was constantly surrounded by strangers. His family, soon after they arrived in Canada, his neighbours, the staff and students at the schools to which he was summoned. He missed his son each night he left for work. Once he followed the boy out of the house but could not match his pace and soon lost sight of him. He returned, breathing heavily. Each trip up the stairs left him similarly breathless.

Raj now thought of joy as fleeting moments that must be seized before they evaporated. But where were these moments? How could they be anticipated and grasped? Could they be seen only in backward glances, their warm glow felt only as memories? Weeks passed, then months. He was always on edge, surveying the world, searching for joy. His son continued to avoid him; his daughter, far away, was equally inaccessible. He broadened his vision across the world and saw religious and racial strife, anger, frustration, resentment. Groups mourning a lost history and others foraging for nobility, stability, humanity. Then he read of a disease that was far away but close to where his daughter was working.

Time was running out.

One night he decided to put his legacy in order. No, not legacy; that was too grand a word. He was thinking of something more mundane, and he recalled a word from his childhood, a *jahaji* bundle; a sack of seeds and religious books and other meagre belongings brought by indentured labourers from India. While he was rummaging through the old boxes in which he stored bills and receipts and the plastic bins into which he consigned mementoes of his past, he thought of his ancestors who had been transported from India, and of his own journey to Canada, and another word came to mind. Transients. I am not tied to any place, he murmured to the boxes. I am a nowherian.

In one of these boxes, he came across two envelopes stuffed with photographs he had brought to Canada. He saw a young man he barely recognized, athletic and vaguely good-looking, on a bench at the local university, at a beach, glancing over his shoulder at a mountain, posing with a cricket bat on the bonnet of a restored Triumph Spitfire. And briefly, briefly, he felt the tiny ruffle of joy he'd been searching for the last eight months. But then he considered all that was lost, and the joy faded.

Raj desperately wished to stir that brief jubilation so he returned to the photographs during the week, and one night as his son was leaving for work, the boy glanced at the kitchen table and asked about the man in the photographs. He pointed to his chest, noting the disbelief on his son's face. Yes, that is me, he wanted to say. This dried-up, old man standing before you. Later in the day, he stood before his bedroom mirror and observed his downturned lips, the sunken cheeks, his hooded eyelids, and his weak eyes that signified his losses; everything he was mourning, and he understood his son's skepticism.

Because he could locate nothing of value in the second half of his life, he began to roam around even more to the first. He started slowly, in the dead of winter, to conjure up this imagined place of lush cane and cocoa, and bamboo groves, and coconut trees leading to coral reefs and pristine beaches, and stalls overflowing with fruits, deep red and striking yellow. He had written, as a young man, poems to represent this view, and although they were simple and derivative, they were published in the local newspaper.

Spliced into his tropical paradise were the women with whom he had brief flings. Teachers, tellers, cashiers, university students whose names he could no longer remember. He recalled little snippets of their faces and bodies, these women all in their twenties. He did not consider that they too would have been bruised by the passing years and these memories were just as fraudulent as those he conjured about himself. Nor did he acknowledge that it was he who had casually and indifferently broken off these relationships. From habit, he ignored everything that was not amenable to this carefree and joyful time.

If Raj had stepped back from this rearrangement of his past, he would have seen that this was not the first occasion he had created a fretwork world from appealing images. Almost three decades earlier, he summoned a place he had put together from calendars displaying apples and pink chubby-cheeked children and Christmas cards with cottages surrounded by snow-capped fir and pine. If he had stepped back even further, he would have noticed that his new pastiche was just as illusive as the first, because missing from the backward reconstruction of his island paradise were all that led him to leave. If his fantasy island was constrained by reality, he would not have awakened one morning with the determination to retrieve what was lost. He would not have visited his bank, his lawyer, and a travel agent the following weeks to cement his plan. He might have spotted in his son traces of curiosity and concern. And when he did notice this, it was too late; everything was set in place.

During his last week in Canada, Raj wanted to apologize to his son but did not know how to begin and what he should say. He also had no real idea as to what exactly he was apologizing for. In those last days he moved to the murky realization that he had been so wrapped in his own losses he had ignored the pain of his children. For instance, even though his father had been as distant as he was, he never felt unloved because he grew up in a village where the inhabitants operated like an extended family. Still, he convinced himself that he was not a bad father but an indifferent one.

His son was at work on the day of his flight. In the taxi and later in the departure lounge, Raj's mind was not fixed on breaking off associations but on reordering his memories to create a semblance of continuity. For the first time he was looking forward. So he did not consider his son's shock at the suddenness of his departure; rather he was convinced the boy would be satisfied with the property in Whitby, the transfer and deed left on the kitchen table. He had taken little because he believed everything he would need was at his destination.

"Travelling light?" the check-in officer asked him, and he was about to utter a foreign word but she had already turned away. On the plane, he fell asleep and dreamed of a farm with green rolling hills. It was familiar terrain and when he awoke, he realized it was not from his village but Ponderosa of the *Bonanza* television series. He was comforted when he glanced around and saw the sleeping brown and black faces. The only person on the plane who seemed to be awake was a baby sucking a comforter on a nearby seat. The baby's face pressed against the mother's shoulder looked bloated and disfigured. The comforter fell on the aisle and the baby looked at him accusingly. What am I doing, at my age and with my infirmities, he thought, and momentarily, he felt a twinge of panic.

He turned his attention to the scene outside the window and tried to imagine what his great grandparents must have been thinking on the packed ship that brought them to the Caribbean. He had heard stories of his great grandfather, twelve years old, and his brother, a year older, hiding items of clothing and little things they planned to take to this place, thousands of miles away. They crept away one night with their jahaji bundle, without telling their parents. Maybe they viewed this escape into an uncertain world as an adventure. They had no idea what misery awaited them. I am different, he thought. I am not moving into a new life. I am disappearing quietly into an old one.

Acknowledgements

I would like to thank Mawenzi House, particularly MG Vassanji and Nurjehan Aziz for bringing these stories to life. I would also like to thank Ingrid Ruthig for reading an early draft, and Kav Maharaj for the cover design.

I am immensely grateful to the Canada Council for the Arts, and the Ontario Arts Council for their financial assistance.

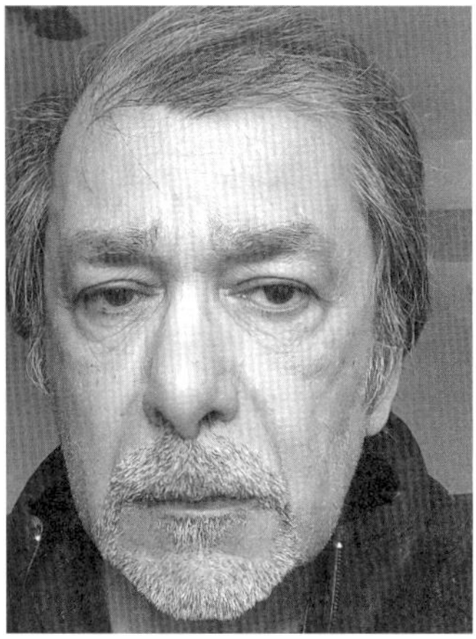

RABINDRANATH MAHARAJ is the author of 10 works of fiction, among them *The Amazing Absorbing Boy* (Trillium Book Award, the Toronto Book Award); *A Perfect Pledge* (Rogers Writers' Trust Fiction Prize, the Commonwealth Writers' Prize finalist); and *Homer in Flight* (Chapters/Books in Canada First Novel Award finalist). He immigrated to Canada from Trinidad in the 1990s, and settled in Ajax, Ontario, where he taught high school and co-founded a literary magazine, *LICHEN*. He has been a writer-in-residence at the Toronto Reference Library, the University of the West Indies, and the University of New Brunswick. Apart from his novels and collections of short stories, he has published in various literary journals and anthologies and written reviews and articles for the *Washington Post*, the *Globe and Mail*, and the *Toronto Star*. He has also written the radio series "Malcolm and Alvin" for CBC Radio, and co-written a screenplay for the film *Malini*.